Places I Never Meant to Be

original stories by censored writers

edited by Judy Blume

Aladdin Paperbacks

New York   London   Toronto   Sydney   Singapore

First Aladdin Paperbacks edition June 2001
Places I Never Meant To Be: Original Stories by Censored Writers © 1999
by Judy Blume
"Baseball Camp" copyright © 1999 by David Klass
"Something Which Is Non-Existent" copyright © 1959 by Norma Klein
"Spear" copyright © 1999 by Julius Lester
"Lie, No Lie" copyright © 1999 by Chris Lynch
"You Come, Too, A-Ron" copyright © 1999 by Harry Mazer
"Meeting the Mugger" copyright © 1999 by Norman Fox Mazer
"The Beast Is in the Labyrinth" copyright © 1999 by Walter Dean Myers
"The Red Dragonfly" copyright © 1999 by Katherine Paterson
"Ashes" copyright © 1999 by Susan Beth Pfeffer
"Going Sentimental" copyright © 1999 by Rachel Vail
"July Saturday" copyright © 1999 by Jacqueline Woodson
"Love and Centipedes" copyright © 1999 by Paul Zindel
Quotes from Norma Klein on pages 195 and 196 were reprinted from *Trust Your
Children: Voices Against Censorship in Children's Literature*, Second Edition, with per-
mission of the publisher. Copyright © 1997 by Neal-Schuman Publishers, Inc.

Aladdin Paperbacks
An imprint of Simon & Schuster
Children's Publishing Division
1230 Avenue of the Americas
New York, NY 10020

Book designed by Lisa Vega
The text for this book is set in Bembo.
Printed and bound in the United States of America

11 12 13 14 15 16 17 18 19 20

The Library of Congress has cataloged the hardcover edition as follows:
Places I never meant to be : original stories by censored writers / edited by Judy
Blume.—1st ed.
p.   cm.
Contents: Introduction/Judy Blume—Meeting the mugger/Norma Fox Mazer—
Spear/Julius Lester—Going sentimental/Rachel Vail—Baseball camp/David Klass—
The red dragonfly/Katherine Paterson—July Saturday/Jacqueline Woodson—Love
and centipedes/Paul Zindel—Lie, no lie/Chris Lynch—You come, too, a-ron/Harry
Mazer—Ashes/Susan Beth Pfeffer—The beast is in the labyrinth/Walter Dean
Myers—Something which is non-existent/Norma Klein.
Summary: A collection of short stories accompanied by short essays on censorship
by twelve authors whose works have been challenged in the past.
ISBN 0-689-82034-8 (hc.)
1. Short stories, American. [1. Short stories.] I. Blume, Judy.
PZ5.P6635   1999
[Fic]—dc21   98-30343   CIP   AC
ISBN 0-689-84258-9 (Aladdin pbk.)

For Leanne Katz, our champion
Your spirit lives on

Some Additional Books by Judy Blume

Are You There God? It's Me, Margaret

Deenie

Then Again, Maybe I Won't

Just As Long As We're Together

Here's To You, Rachel Robinson

Tiger Eyes

Forever

Summer Sisters

Contents

Censorship: A Personal View

by
Judy Blume

When I was growing up I'd heard that if a movie or book was "Banned in Boston" everybody wanted to see it or read it right away. My older brother, for example, went to see such a movie—*The Outlaw,* starring Jane Russell—and I wasn't supposed to tell my mother. I begged him to share what he saw, but he wouldn't. I was intensely curious about the adult world and hated the secrets my parents, and now my brother, kept from me.

A few years later, when I was in fifth grade, my mother was reading a novel called *A Rage to Live,* by John O'Hara, and for the first time (and, as it turned out, the *only* time) in my life, she told me I was never to look at that book, at least not until I was *much* older. Once I knew my mother didn't want me to read it, I figured it must be really interesting!

So, you can imagine how surprised and delighted I was when, as a junior in high school, I found John O'Hara's name on my reading list. Not a specific title by John O'Hara, but *any* title. I didn't waste a minute. I went down to the public library in Elizabeth, New Jersey, that afternoon—a place where I'd spent so many happy hours as a young child, I'd pasted a card pocket on the inside back cover of each book I owned—and looked for *A Rage to Live.* But I couldn't find it. When I asked, the librarian told

---

me *that* book was *restricted*. It was kept in a locked closet, and I couldn't take it out without written permission from my parents.

Aside from my mother's one moment of fear, neither of my parents had ever told me what I could or could not read. They encouraged me to read widely. There were no "Young Adult" novels then. Serious books about teenagers were published as adult novels. It was my mother who handed me *To Kill a Mockingbird* and Anne Frank's *Diary of a Young Girl* when they were first published.

By the time I was twelve I was browsing in the bookshelves flanking the fireplace in our living room where, in my quest to make sense of the world, I discovered J. D. Salinger's *The Catcher in the Rye,* fell in love with the romantic tragedies of Thomas Hardy and the Brontë sisters, and overidentified with "Marjorie Morningstar."

But at the Elizabeth Public Library the librarian didn't care. "Get permission in writing," she told me. When I realized she was not going to let me check out *A Rage to Live,* I was angry. I felt betrayed and held her responsible. It never occurred to me that it might not have been her choice.

At home I complained to my family, and that evening my aunt, the principal of an elementary school, brought me her copy of *A Rage to Live.* I stayed up half the night reading the forbidden book. Yes, it was sexy, but the characters and their story were what kept me turning the pages. Finally, my curiosity (about that book, anyway) was satisfied. Instead of leading me astray, as my mother must have feared, it led me to read everything else I could find by the author.

✻ ✻ ✻

All of which brings me to the question *What is censorship?* If you ask a dozen people you'll get twelve different answers. When I actually looked up the word in *The Concise Columbia Encyclopedia* I found this definition: "[The] official restriction of any expression believed to threaten the political, social, or moral order." My thesaurus lists the following words that can be used in place of *ban* (as in book banning): *Forbid. Prohibit. Restrict.* But what do these words mean to writers and the stories they choose to tell? And what do they mean to readers and the books they choose to read?

* * *

I began to write when I was in my mid-twenties. By then I was married with two small children and desperately in need of creative work. I wrote *Are You There God? It's Me, Margaret* right out of my own experiences and feelings when I was in sixth grade. Controversy wasn't on my mind. I wanted only to write what I knew to be true. I wanted to write the best, the most honest books I could, the kinds of books I would have liked to read when I was younger. If someone had told me then I would become one of the most banned writers in America, I'd have laughed.

When *Margaret* was published in 1970 I gave three copies to my children's elementary school but the books never reached the shelves. The male principal decided on his own that they were inappropriate for elementary school readers because of the discussion of menstruation (never mind how many fifth- and sixth-grade girls already had their periods). Then one night the phone rang and a woman asked if I was the one who had written *that* book. When I replied that I was, she called me a communist and hung up. I never did figure out if she equated communism with menstruation or religion.

In that decade I wrote thirteen other books: eleven for young readers, one for teenagers, and one for adults. My publishers were protective of me during those years and didn't necessarily share negative comments about my work. They believed if I didn't know some individuals were upset by my books, I wouldn't be intimidated.

Of course, they couldn't keep the occasional anecdote from reaching me: the mother who admitted she'd cut two pages out of *Then Again, Maybe I Won't* rather than allow her almost thirteen-year-old son to read about wet dreams. Or the young librarian who'd been instructed by her male principal to keep *Deenie* off the shelf because in the book, Deenie masturbates. "It would be different if it were about a boy," he'd told her. "That would be normal."

The stories go on and on but really, I wasn't that concerned. There was no organized effort to ban my books or any other books, none that I knew of, anyway. The seventies were a good decade for writers and readers. Many of us came of age during those years, writing from our hearts and guts, finding editors and publishers who believed in us, who willingly took risks to help us find our audience. We were free to write about real kids in the real world. Kids with feelings and emotions, kids with real families, kids like we once were. And young readers gobbled up our books, hungry for characters with whom they could identify, including my own daughter and son, who had become avid readers. No mother could have been more proud to see the tradition of family reading passed on to the next generation.

*　*　*

Then, almost overnight, following the presidential election of 1980, the censors crawled out of the woodwork, organized and determined. Not only would they decide what *their* children could read but what *all* children could read. It was the beginning of the decade that wouldn't go away, that still won't go away almost twenty years later. Suddenly books were seen as dangerous to young minds. Thinking was seen as dangerous, unless those thoughts were approved by groups like the Moral Majority, who believed with certainty they knew what was best for everyone.

So now we had individual parents running into schools, waving books, demanding their removal—books they hadn't read except for certain passages. Most often their objections had to do with language, sexuality, and something called "lack of moral tone."

Those who were most active in trying to ban books came from the "religious right" but the impulse to censor spread like a contagious disease. Other parents, confused and uncertain, were happy to jump on the bandwagon. Book banning satisfied their need to feel in control of their children's lives. Those who censored were easily frightened. They were afraid of exposing their children to ideas different from their own. Afraid to answer children's questions or talk with them about sensitive subjects. And they were suspicious. They believed if kids liked a book, it must be dangerous.

Too few schools had policies in place enabling them to deal with challenged materials. So what happened? The domino effect. School administrators sent down the word: Anything that could be seen as controversial had to go. Often books were quietly removed from school libraries and classrooms or, if seen as potential troublemakers, were never purchased in the first place. These decisions were based not on what was best for the students, but what would *not* offend the censors.

I found myself at the center of the storm. My books were being challenged daily, often placed on *restricted* shelves (shades of Elizabeth, New Jersey, in 1955) and sometimes removed. A friend was handed a pamphlet outside a supermarket urging parents to rid their schools and libraries of Judy Blume books. Never once did the pamphlet suggest the books actually be read. Of course I wasn't the only target. Across the country, the Sex Police and the Language Police were thumbing through books at record speed, looking for illustrations, words or phrases that, taken out of context, could be used as evidence against them.

Puberty became a dirty word, as if children who didn't read about it wouldn't know about it, and if they didn't know about it, it would never happen.

The Moral Tone Brigade attacked *Blubber* (a story of victimization in the classroom) with a vengeance because, as they saw it, in this book evil goes unpunished. As if kids need to be hit over the head, as if they don't get *it* without having the message spelled out for them.

I had letters from angry parents accusing me of ruining Christmas because of a chapter in *Superfudge* called "Santa Who?" Some sent lists showing me how easily I could have substituted one word for another: *meanie* for *bitch; darn* for *damn; nasty* for *ass.* More words taken out of context. A teacher wrote to say she blacked out offending words and passages with a felt-tip marker. Perhaps most shocking of all was a letter from a nine-year-old addressed to *Jew*dy Blume telling me I had no right to write about Jewish angels in *Starring Sally J. Freedman as Herself.*

My worst moment came when I was working with my editor on the manuscript of *Tiger Eyes* (the story of a fifteen-year-old girl, Davey, whose beloved father dies suddenly and violently). When we came to the scene in which Davey allows herself to *feel* again after months of numbness following her father's death, I saw that a few lines alluding to masturbation had been circled. My editor put down his pencil and faced me. "We want this book to reach as many readers as possible, don't we?" he asked.

I felt my face grow hot, my stomach clench. This was the same editor who had worked with me on *Are You There God? It's Me, Margaret; Then Again, Maybe I Won't; Deenie; Blubber; Forever*— always encouraging, always supportive. The scene was psychologically sound, he assured me, and delicately handled. But it also spelled trouble. I got the message. If you leave in those lines, the censors will come after this book. Librarians and teachers won't buy it. Book clubs won't take it. Everyone is too scared. The political climate has changed.

I tried to make a case for why that brief moment in Davey's life was important. He asked me *how* important? Important enough to keep the book from reaching its audience? I willed myself not to give in to the tears of frustration and disappointment I felt coming. I thought about the ways a writer brings a character to life on the page, the same way an artist brings a face to life on canvas— through a series of brush strokes, each detail adding to the others, until we see the essence of the person. I floundered, uncertain. Ultimately, not strong enough or brave enough to defy the editor I trusted and respected, I caved in and took out those lines. I still remember how alone I felt at that moment.

*   *   *

What effect does this climate have on a writer? *Chilling.* It's easy to become discouraged, to second-guess everything you write. There seemed to be no one to stand up to the censors. No group as organized as they were; none I knew of, anyway. I've never forgiven myself for caving in to editorial pressure based on fear, for playing into the hands of the censors. I knew then it was all over for me unless I took a stand. So I began to speak out about my experiences. And once I did, I found that I wasn't as alone as I'd thought.

* * *

My life changed when I learned about the National Coalition Against Censorship (NCAC) and met Leanne Katz, the tiny dynamo who was its first and longtime director. Leanne's intelligence, her wit, her strong commitment to the First Amendment and helping those who were out on a limb trying to defend it, made her my hero. Every day she worked with the teachers, librarians, parents and students caught in the cross fire. Many put themselves and their jobs on the line fighting for what they believed in.

In Panama City, Florida, junior high school teacher Gloria Pipkin's award-winning English program was targeted by the censors for using Young Adult literature that was *depressing, vulgar and immoral,* specifically *I Am the Cheese,* by Robert Cormier, and *About David,* by Susan Beth Pfeffer.

A year later, when a new book selection policy was introduced forbidding vulgar, obscene and sexually related materials, the school superintendent zealously applied it to remove more than sixty-five books, many of them classics, from the curriculum and classroom libraries. They included *To Kill a Mockingbird,*

The Red Badge of Courage, The Great Gatsby, Wuthering Heights, and Of Mice and Men. Also banned were Shakespeare's Hamlet, King Lear, The Merchant of Venice and Twelfth Night.

Gloria Pipkin fought a five-year battle, jeopardizing her job and personal safety (she and the reporter covering the story received death threats) to help reinstate the books. Eventually, the professional isolation as well as the watered-down curriculum led her to resign. She remains without a teaching position.

Claudia Johnson, Florida State University professor and parent, also defended classic books by Aristophanes and Chaucer against a censor who condemned them for promoting "women's lib and pornography." She went on to fight other battles—in defense of John Steinbeck's Of Mice and Men, and a student performance of Lorraine Hansberry's A Raisin in the Sun.

English teacher Cecilia Lacks was fired by a high school in St. Louis for permitting her creative writing students to express themselves in the language they heard and used outside of school everyday. In the court case that followed, many of her students testified on their teacher's behalf. Though she won her case, the decision was eventually reversed and at this time Lacks is still without a job.

Colorado English teacher Alfred Wilder was fired for teaching a classic film about fascism, Bernardo Bertolucci's 1900.

And in Rib Lake, Wisconsin, guidance counselor Mike Dishnow was fired for writing critically of the Board of Education's decision to ban my book Forever from the junior high school library. Ultimately he won a court settlement, but by then his life had been turned upside down.

. And these are just a few examples.

∗ ∗ ∗

This obsession with banning books continues into the 21st century. Today it is not only Sex, Swear Words and Lack of Moral Tone—it is Evil, which, according to the censors, can be found lurking everywhere. Stories about Halloween, witches, and devils are all suspect for promoting Satanism. *Romeo and Juliet* is under fire for promoting suicide; Madeleine L'Engle's *A Wrinkle in Time*, for promoting New Age-ism. If the censors had their way it would be good-bye to Shakespeare as well as science fiction. There's not an *ism* you can think of that's not bringing some book to the battlefield.

What I worry about most is the loss to young people. If no one speaks out for them, if they don't speak out for themselves, all they'll get for required reading will be the most bland books available. And instead of finding the information they need at the library, instead of finding the novels that illuminate life, they will find only those materials to which nobody could possibly object.

Some people would like to rate books in schools and libraries the way they rate movies: G, PG, R, X, or even more explicitly. But according to whose standards would the books be rated? I don't know about you but I don't want anyone rating my books or the books my children or grandchildren choose to read. We can make our own decisions, thank you. Be wary of the censors' code words—*family friendly; family values; excellence in education.* As if the rest of us don't want excellence in education, as if we don't have our own family values, as if libraries haven't always been family-friendly places!

And the demands are not all coming from the religious right. No . . . the urge to decide not only what's right for their kids but for all kids has caught on with others across the political spectrum. Each year *Huckleberry Finn* is challenged and sometimes removed from the classroom because, to some, its language, which includes racial epithets, is offensive. Better to acknowledge the language, bring it out in the open, and discuss why the book remains important than to ban it. Teachers and parents can talk with their students and children about any book considered controversial.

I gave a friend's child one of my favorite picture books, James Marshall's *The Stupids Step Out*, and was amazed when she said, "I'm sorry, but we can't accept that book. My children are not permitted to use that word. Ever. It should be changed to 'The Sillies Step Out.' " I may not agree, but I have to respect this woman's right to keep that book from her child as long as she isn't trying to keep it from other people's children. Still, I can't help lamenting the lack of humor in her decision. *The Stupids Step Out* is a very funny book. Instead of banning it from her home, I wish she could have used it as an opportunity to talk with her child about why she felt the way she did, about why she never wanted to hear her child call anyone *stupid*. Even very young children can understand. So many adults are exhausting themselves worrying about other people corrupting their children with books, they're turning kids off to reading instead of turning them on.

In this age of censorship I mourn the loss of books that will never be written, I mourn the voices that will be silenced—writers' voices, teachers' voices, students' voices—and all because of fear. How many have resorted to self-censorship? How many are saying to themselves, "Nope . . . can't write about that. Can't teach that book. Can't have that book in our collection. Can't let my student write that editorial in the school paper."

* * *

This book is dedicated to Leanne Katz to commemorate a life spent trying to prevent voices from being silenced. (Leanne died in 1997.) It is our way of thanking her and NCAC for their hard and valuable work, which continues today under the able direction of Joan Bertin and her small staff of dedicated coworkers. All the royalties from the sale of this book will go directly to NCAC to benefit their work.

Many censored writers are missing from this collection: Maya Angelou, Stephen King, Lois Lowry, Margaret Atwood, Alice Walker, Richard Peck, Bruce Coville, Ken Follett, Kurt Vonnegut, J. D. Salinger, Shel Silverstein, the anonymous author of *Go Ask Alice,* to name just a few. Some, like my friend, Robert Cormier, whose *I Am the Cheese* started the fracas in Panama City, say they just can't write short stories. I know what they mean. I've never been a short-story writer either. Others were trying to meet deadlines and weren't able to fit this project into their busy schedules. But almost all have joined us in spirit.

I'm grateful to the outstanding writers who have contributed to this anthology. They've come up with a fascinating group of characters. In a wry story of teenage love, you'll meet a couple who have been best friends for years, deciding the time is right to lose their virginity. In another story, the unforgettable Sarabeth takes off one night when the going gets tough at home, only to find herself in the most threatening situation of her life. There is John, a college student torn between the opportunities his education affords and his responsibilities to his family. And a group of teenage boys spending their summer vacation at baseball camp, where they meet up with an unspeakably cruel coach. You'll be transported from a story of romantic infatuation in Japan to the wacky world of Tuesday Racinski, who has no choice but to use her supernatural powers to zap Miss Popularity. Whether the situation is dead serious or wildly funny, all of these characters find themselves in places they never meant to be.

Aside from being good storytellers, what these writers have in common is that somewhere along the way their work has been challenged by an individual or group wanting to *forbid, prohibit or restrict* the books they have written. In some cases the censors have been successful; in others, sanity has prevailed. Following each story the writer shares his/her personal experiences and feelings about censorship. Remember, *if you ask a dozen people what censorship means, you'll get twelve different answers.*

* * *

The bottom line is, censorship happens, often when you least expect it. It's not just about the book you may want to read but about the book your classmate might want to read. It's not just about teachers and librarians at other schools who might find themselves in job-threatening situations—it could happen at your school. Your favorite teacher, the one who made literature come alive for you, the one who helped you find exactly the book you needed when you were curious, or hurting, the one who was there to listen to you when you felt alone, could become the next target.

And what can you do if censorship hits close to home?

The first step is awareness. Become informed. Take a stand. Work with the adults in your community. Don't try to do it on your own. Contact one or more of the following support groups immediately.

National Coalition Against Censorship
275 Seventh Avenue
New York, New York 10001
Tel.: 212-807-6222
Fax: 212-807-6245
E-mail: ncac@netcom.com
Web site: www.ncac.org

Office for Intellectual Freedom
American Library Association
Judith Krug, Director
50 East Huron Street
Chicago, Illinois 60611
Tel.: 800-545-2433, ext.: 4222
Fax: 312-280-4227
E-mail: jkrug@ala.org
Web site: www.ala.org/oif.html

People for the American Way
Attn: Pia Sumler
2000 M Street NW, Suite 400
Washington, D.C. 20036
Tel.: 202-467-4999
Fax: 202-293-2672
Web site: www.pfaw.org

They will help you help yourself. Get the local newspaper involved. Censors hate publicity. So do school boards. If you don't take a stand, others will eagerly make decisions that affect your First Amendment rights. Make sure you know what those rights are.

* * *

A word of warning to anyone who writes or wants to write: There is no predicting the censor. No telling what will be seen as controversial tomorrow. I've talked with writers who have told me, "Oh . . . I don't write the kinds of stories you do. I write for younger children. My work will never be attacked," only to find themselves under fire the next day.

So write honestly. Write from deep inside. Leanne used to say, "It's your job to write as well as you can, Judy. It's my job to defend what you've written."

But Leanne couldn't do it on her own. No one can. It's up to all of us.

A Letter from Joan Bertin, Executive Director, National Coalition Against Censorship

Here at the National Coalition Against Censorship (NCAC) we receive hundreds of calls about censorship every year, from students and parents, teachers and librarians, artists, writers, and others. We provide information and advice, resources and referrals. We work with other First Amendment advocacy groups to educate the public about the importance of free speech and to publicize instances of censorship so that people who believe in the value of free expression will know when and where to make their voices heard.

Our newsletter, *Censorship News*, is published four times a year and keeps our readers informed about important censorship issues. Sometimes we provide testimony in Congress or state legislatures, and we hold public meetings and seminars on First Amendment issues, often having to do with students' rights. Many of our materials are now available on our Web site—www.ncac.org.

Most people say they believe in the First Amendment, but when you get down to specifics it's clear that many people don't really understand it. They want the First Amendment to protect the material *they* like, but not necessarily what *you* like. Some people object to sex or violence, others are offended by what they consider to be disrespectful of religion, or parental authority, or the government. Some people object to nudity in art, even to Michelangelo's masterpiece, *David*.

Parents and others who complain often do so out of deep beliefs or convictions, and often in an effort to "protect" young people from influences they believe are harmful. Of course, no one wants to subject students to harmful influences. But given the wide range of opinion, if everyone had the right to veto what he or she didn't like, nothing much would be left.

Those of us who oppose censorship believe that reading about something is a safe way to explore and understand it, and that it is the best way to prepare young people to deal with the issues they will face, both in school and later in life. It's true that some material is "offensive"—but to know how to respond to it, we need to understand it. The first step in that process is to read and talk about it with an informed and responsible adult, like a teacher or parent. For this reason, we think that school *should* be the place where students are able to read about and discuss controversial or difficult issues.

Unfortunately, the censors are bold and busy these days. Their focus is often on what students read, see and hear in schools. Therefore, we're especially grateful to the writers who have contributed stories to this wonderful collection, and for their frank discussions of the ways in which censorship has affected their work and lives. And we thank them for donating all of the royalties from the sale of this book to NCAC, to further our anticensorship work. We also thank Simon & Schuster for publishing this book and for their own contribution to NCAC, and Judy Blume, a tireless advocate for free expression.

I stood at the edge of the highway. It was dark and raining. Cars streamed past. In a lull, I ran across. On the other side, I walked through a field and onto the road around the quarry, and then I kept walking. I ended up in the city, in the rain, in a neighborhood I didn't know. These were all things Mom would have said showed a lack of thought, and she would have been right. As soon as I heard the footsteps behind me, I knew I was in trouble, and it was her name that came to my lips. "Mom," I whispered.

Meeting the Mugger

by
Norma Fox Mazer

1. The Argument

For as long as I could remember, my mother had been giving me advice and telling me things about life so that I wouldn't, as she said, make the same mistakes she had. "I want you to have a better time of it than I did." By which she meant a life that was not so difficult, so short on money, and so long on work. "Life is like a river, sweetie pie," she said. "There are times when it's raging and all you can do is hang on. And times when it's calm, and you float in it and let it take you along and you feel the sun on your face, and those are the times you treasure. That's what I do, anyway, or try to. Are you listening, Sarabeth?"

No, I wasn't. Lately, I had felt impatient with her and her advice, so sometimes I took it in and sometimes I didn't. I can see now that she gave me good advice, but more than that, I can see that with everything she said she was trying to protect me from something else, something bigger, something she didn't even want to name.

She couldn't take advice, herself, though. Maybe too much had happened to her and she thought no one could tell her anything she didn't already know. She wouldn't listen to me, certainly. I have to say that wasn't the reason I ran out of the house that night, but now it seems to figure in my thinking. I believe it added to my impatience with her and was one step, at least, in what happened.

The short version of that night: Mom and I were having an argument. Leo came over and put in his two cents. He was saying this, Mom was saying that. They were both on me, and I walked out.

Now, the long version: Mom and I were, or maybe we weren't, having an argument. It wasn't a big yelling thing. We were at the kitchen table, she was folding laundry, and I was doing homework. Tobias was purring in my lap. Suddenly Mom stood up, pulled down her jeans, and showed me a spot on her thigh that looked like a huge, mossy freckle. "What do you think of that?" she asked

"What is it?"

"Some weird skin thing, probably from getting my hands in all those nasty cleaning chemicals."

"That's not your hands. Are you going to see a doctor?"

"Forget it. I have to work two days to make enough money for an office visit. Which will only come to nothing, anyway."

"How do you know that?" I said.

"Oh, I know!" She showed me a hard lump on her forefinger. "See that? What is it?" She didn't wait for an answer. "Calcium deposit. I read about it in a magazine. Did I have to pay a doctor to tell me that?" Then, slick as could be, she changed the subject. "You're almost fifteen. Can you believe it?"

"I'm fourteen, Mom. My birthday isn't for eight months."

"I was that age when I got pregnant with you."

"You weren't fourteen, Mom!"

"Fifteen. I was fifteen. Sixteen, when I had you."

I petted Tobias. I knew the whole story. I could recite it with her, all the phrases, all the warnings. "Way too young to have sex or a baby," I whispered into Tobias's ear.

"Way too young to have sex or a baby. I was crazy for your father, loved him, but it wasn't enough. Like that song says, What's love got to do with anything? The fact that we got married—I used to think that made it all perfect and right. Are you listening?"

"Yes. You got the lyric wrong."

"If he hadn't been killed in that stupid, stupid accident—"

"I know."

"I want to emphasize to you that to have sex so young is really and truly crazy."

"I know."

"It's not just about babies, anymore. It's not just about, will he marry you or do you have to consider an abortion, it's about your life, your actual life. AIDS."

"Mom, I know!" I looked down at Tobias. He was like a big white-and-orange pillow in my lap.

"Call me out of date, whatever, but I want you to take everything slowly. Boys, dating—"

"Why don't you trust me? You worry all the time that I'm going to do something wrong. I have good sense! You've been telling me the same stuff for years. I'm not dumb. I get it!"

She slapped a sheet down on the pile of laundry. "You've changed. I don't know when it happened. We used to have such good talks—I could say anything to you. Is something bothering you?"

"No." Even if it was, like my flat chest and no boy interested, I wouldn't talk about it to her, because she'd just grimace or laugh. *Is that all? If that's the worst problem you ever have in your life, count yourself lucky!*

"You're a teenager now, and what with hormones and peer pressure—"

"Ugh! Stop! Don't talk to me like that. It makes me want to vomit. You sound like a TV show." I was yelling. Tobias slipped off my lap and hid under a chair. "I'm tired of hearing about boys and sex and hormones!"

That was the line Leo came in on. Actually, Leo and Pepper. Leo, with his bowed legs, his big, handsome head, his big shout. "Here's Leo, folks!" As if there should be an instant celebration.

"Leo, baby," Mom said. Then she saw Pepper.

"This is my friend Pepper Rudman," Leo said.

Pepper's fingers were covered with silver rings. She was wearing a long loose skirt under a black vest and jacket. She was somebody you would look at a second time.

Mom glanced down at herself. Jeans, sneakers, a plaid shirt. Pepper smiled at me. I turned a page in my algebra book, and acted as if I were working out a tough problem. Maybe so. I scribbled Leo + Pepper = X? He was Mom's boyfriend.

He got milk from the refrigerator and poured himself a glass. We all watched. "You guys busy or what?" he said to Mom. "In the mood for company?"

"Not busy," Mom said. "Just having a little argument with my teenage daughter."

They all laughed. I hated their laughter, hated that Mom talked in that we-grown-ups-know-about-kids voice. Leo squeezed Mom's arm. "You two!" As if we were this little old comedy team. "Don't let this girl of yours put anything over on you, Janie."

"Be quiet, Leo!" I said.

"Sarabeth's mad," Leo said. "Uh-oh. Watch out."

"I'm not mad, Leo."

"You are. You're mad. She's mad, Pepper."

Pepper smiled in a certain way, as if she was thinking her own thoughts about us, about me and Mom. I closed my notebook. "I am not mad." I didn't know who I was talking to, Pepper, Mom, or Leo. I kept my voice even. "Why don't you go away now and come back some other time, Leo?"

He smirked at me with his upper lip pulled back. "You're growing up and getting quite the temper, aren't you?"

"Sometimes she gets mad the moment I open my mouth," Mom said.

"Uh-huh," Leo said knowingly. Pepper smiled again in that secret way.

Suddenly I went from being rational to crazy. I shouted, "I can't stand this!" I slammed my algebra book shut. Tobias jumped back in my lap and bit my hair trying to comfort me. I dumped him, grabbed my jacket, and ran out.

2. The Mugger

I stood at the edge of the highway. It was dark and raining. Cars streamed past, their lights slanting into the wet air. In a lull, I ran across. On the other side, I walked through a field, and onto the road around the quarry, and then I kept on walking. I ended up in the city, in the rain, in a neighborhood I didn't know. These were all things Mom would have said showed a lack of thought, and she would have been right. As soon as I heard the footsteps behind me, I knew I was in trouble, and it was her name that came to my lips. "Mom," I whispered.

It was Saturday night and the street was empty of people and cars. There were a few stores with shuttered windows, some old boarded-up warehouses. A dog prowling behind a wire fence growled and laid back his ears. He resembled a coyote—that lean, skinny frame. I walked faster. The dog kept pace with me, rumbling in his throat. Behind me, the footsteps grew closer.

I prayed to see someone else, anyone: It could be an old guy who could hardly totter, but I'd be so glad, I'd kiss him a hundred times. Ahead, at the corner, there was a street lamp. Rain fell straight down under the light. If I turned there, maybe I'd see a house, lights, cars, people. The thought of it sent me into a run.

The footsteps came after me. Panting, I glanced back. A guy in a hooded jacket, the hood half off. A lot of hair. The face impressed itself on me, eyes almost blank in their intensity. I should never have looked; it slowed me down. He caught me and grabbed the back of my jacket. "Give it to me!" he said.

Only it wasn't "he." It was a girl, and for a moment, I was relieved. "I don't have any money!" I pulled out my pockets to show her I was telling the truth.

"Give it to me." She had a tight, mean voice. She yanked at my sleeve. "Give me the jacket!"

"Uh . . . this?" I almost laughed. I fumbled with the zipper. Would she still want it if I told her that Mom had bought it in a thrift shop? "Look at this, Sarabeth! I scored!" Mom had been thrilled. A designer name, perfect condition, half a dozen pockets and zippers.

"Hurry up." She had something in her hand—a knife, or maybe a razor. She motioned for me to drop the jacket on the sidewalk. I did. Light from the street lamp glanced off the knife. I noticed this. I noticed that I was noticing it, and other things, too, like how the lumps of her breasts were pushing out her sweatshirt. She wasn't flat chested like me. I felt weirdly proud of this observation, reasoning that this proved how calm I was.

"Turn around." She shoved me into a wall. The bricks were wet and smelled burned. "You stay there," she said in that mean, wound-up voice.

"Okay," I said. Or maybe I didn't say it, because she yelled, "Did you hear what I said? You stay there!"

"Okay."

"You stay there or I'll come back and get you." She sounded tired. Something pressed into my back, slid hard down my spine. "You gonna stay there?"

"Yes."

"You better, and I mean it."

I stood with my face in the bricks. I heard her moving away. I wanted to turn around, but I was afraid she was tricking me. My legs felt strange, weak, like the legs of someone old. When I finally turned, she was gone and the street was empty again.

3. The Waiting-for-Me Party

Mom greeted me at the door. "Where the hell were you?"

I was soaked, shivering. I grabbed a sweater from the hook by the door and threw it over my shoulders. All the way home, running, I had been talking to Mom, telling her about the mugging, the girl, the knife, telling her everything. *It was the worst thing that ever happened to me.* But now, I said nothing.

Over her shoulder I saw Leo and Pepper, Mrs. Prang from Number Six across the way, and old Mr. Symbarska from Number Eighteen. Whenever Mr. Symbarska saw me around the trailer park he would say, "You gonna be my sweetheart?" Like I was four, instead of fourteen.

They were all crowded around the table. The cloth was lit-
tered with cake crumbs and napkins. It looked as if they'd been
having a party. A waiting-for-Sarabeth party.

I took off my sneakers and socks. I dried my feet with a dish
towel, and they all watched as if I was the party's featured attrac-
tion. Watch Sarabeth bend over! See her dry her feet! Look at
those smart toes!

"Do you know what time it is?" my mother said. "You've
been gone over three hours."

"How could you do that to your mother?" Mrs. Prang said.
She had glittery black hair, a glittery white smile. Like Mom, she
had one daughter, but Melissa was older than me and lived in
Aberdeen, Texas.

"Could you say something?" Leo said. "Sarabeth, at least apologize to your mother."

"Your poor mother!" Mrs. Prang said. "She was so worried. I
thought you were one of the good ones. I thought better of
you."

"Mamas worry," Mr. Symbarska agreed.

Was he consoling me, or scolding me? Only Pepper didn't say
anything. Her head went left, right . . . left, right. . . .

"You walked out," Mom said. "You just walked out. Bang! You
were gone." Her face had that squinty look it got when she was
totally fried. "What were you thinking of, Sarabeth? I was ready
to call the police!"

I sat down. My eyes hurt from the light. It seemed as if even
the walls were glaring at me. I stared at the tablecloth. There was
a tea stain on the edge, the same shape as New York State. I
picked out where we lived right in the center.

"Sarabeth!" Leo's voice boomed. "Answer your mother, for

crying out loud. You can't just sit there like a lump. Speak," he ordered. "You've got to get responsible."

"He's right." Mrs. Prang wagged her finger at me. "The man is ab-so-lutely right."

"Right, right, right," Mr. Symbarska agreed.

It was like a madhouse, and then it got worse. Mr. Symbarska broke into song. "Make up, make up," he sang. "You and your mom must make up." Pepper giggled, the first sound out of her.

"You like my song? You make me happy," he sang. "You are my sunny sunshine when skies are gray, my sunny sunshine every day."

I sank lower in the chair and eyed the piece of cake that was left on his plate. I was hungry. Famished, actually.

"Why are you such a mess, Sarabeth?" Leo said. "Did you fall down or something? Your face is all scratched up."

Mom leaned toward me, as if she were only really seeing me now. "Where's your jacket?" she said. "Didn't you go out with your jacket? And your face—Leo's right. What happened to your face."

I still didn't speak. I couldn't. I stepped over Leo's feet and went into my room.

4. Talking to Leo

I heard the kitchen door opening, the creaky noise it made. I heard their voices like a big rush of water. "Good night . . . good night . . . thanks for coming over." That was Mom. "Goodnight, darling." Mrs. Prang. Mr. Symbarska, still singing. Pepper murmuring. Leo laughing, a snort like a donkey. I hadn't apologized to Mom, like he said I should, but I hadn't stepped on his feet,

----

either. Too bad. He had spoken to me as if I were his dog. "Speak, Sarabeth!"

Speak, Leo! Who is this Pepper Rudman? I thought you were Mom's boyfriend. You sure are a disloyal type!

I reached around and touched my back. My shirt was torn and sticky, my skin burned under my fingers. "Tobias," I called. Where was he? I wanted him a lot just then, or maybe I wanted something else. Maybe I just wanted to cry. I looked out the window. Leo and Pepper were walking toward his car. "Leo!" I yelled suddenly. "Leo, come over here."

"Is that you, Sarabeth?" He came to the window.

"Leo." I didn't know what I was going to say. "Do you like that jacket you're wearing?" It was black, with slanted pockets.

"Sure," he said. "It's okay."

"Yes or no, Leo, do you like it or don't you?"

He shielded his eyes. "What does it matter? It's just an old jacket."

"It matters, Leo. Everything matters." My voice quivered.

"Hey. You're right. You feeling better?"

"I'm fine."

"So, go tell Jane where you were. It'll be okay, don't worry."

"I never worry." What a lie. "Who is Pepper Rudman, anyway?"

"A friend. She teaches at Community College. What happened to you tonight? Where'd you go? Or were you hanging around here the whole time, just getting your mother worked up?"

Did he really think I'd pull a stunt like that? "Good-bye, Leo!" I shut the window in his face.

"Sarabeth, hey—"

I yanked down the shade. It made that ripping sound that meant the spring had unwound.

5. Mom and Me

Mom brought me a tuna sandwich. Lots of mayo, the way I liked it. She sat in the rocker and watched me eat. "So what's going on?" she said, finally.

I licked mayo off my fingers. "Are you getting sick, mom?" Her skin was sort of greenish looking.

"Never mind me. Just tell me what happened to you tonight."

"It was stupid." I looked up at the ceiling. "Don't freak, okay? I was walking on this street, and a girl with a knife—"

"A girl with a knife?"

"I didn't know she had it, until she grabbed me. She took my jacket, and I think she did something to my back." I turned to show her.

"She cut you!" Mom said. "Oh my god! She cut you!" She ran out.

I was glad I couldn't see the cut. I hate being cut. Even a little paper cut, the kind you get when you slide your finger over the edge of a sheet of paper, affects me, as if that tiny break in the skin reveals too much, how fragile a barrier skin is, how the life beneath it, blood and bones, can be reached so easily, and how effortlessly anyone can be separated from life.

"Is it bad?" I asked when Mom came back.

"Your shirt is history." She was smoothing on some kind of first-aid cream. She wrapped me in a blanket and sat down next to me.

"I didn't feel anything when she did it," I said. "I was so calm, Mom. I could have started a conversation with her, asked her where she went to school, why she had to do this."

"Little bitch. I'd like to get my hands on her."

"She was scared, Mom. I think she was more scared, in a way, than I was."

"You can feel sorry for her, but I don't. I sure don't! She cut you, she could have really hurt you."

Mom put her arms around me, and I let myself lean against her, let myself go heavy, as if she were still my big mommy, instead of our being the same size now. It was sweet. It was heavenly. For the first time in hours, I felt okay.

We sat there like that for a long time, and it was the way it used to be, the two of us close, so close, as close as if we were a single organism, as if we had come from the same source and could never be torn apart.

"I was mugged," I said. "Mugged and cut. It's the worst thing that ever happened to me." I started to cry.

"Shh. Shh, baby," Mom said. "Honey baby . . . sweetie pie." She rocked me and held me tighter.

6. The Morning As Usual

I made myself a cup of coffee milk and sat down. "Is that all you're eating for breakfast?" Mom said.

"I'm not hungry."

"You need food to have your brains work right."

"My brains work okay." It was the same conversation we had every morning. I could hardly believe it.

"You only had a *B* in math last term." She put half a grapefruit in front of me. "Is that a lump on your forehead?" She took my chin in her hands. "Did that girl do that, too?"

I nodded and touched the lump gingerly. It had popped out overnight.

"We're a pair," Mom said. "You with your lump, me with mine." She got an ice pack from the freezer and gave it to me. "That should take the swelling down."

"Mom, what about you and Leo? Is he dumping you?"

"Thanks, Sarabeth, that's a really nice way to put it."

"Is he?"

She shrugged. "I don't know. I guess ... yeah, I guess he is. Big news, huh?"

I pressed the ice pack against my forehead. "I hate him."

"Look, it happens. You can't go nuts about things you can't control."

"Maybe," I said. I put on my sweater and slung my backpack over my shoulder.

"Is that all you're wearing?" she said. "It's cold outside."

"I don't have a jacket, remember?" I said. She wanted me to take hers. I said no. She insisted. I said no again. "If one of us is going to be cold, it can be me," I said. "I'm younger and stronger."

That made her mad and we almost got into an argument again.

"I'll take it," I said, "if you go to a doctor about that freckle thing on your leg." She nodded. She must have been more worried about it than she'd let on. "You'll make an appointment today?" I said, and she nodded again.

I put on her jacket, and we went out the door together. The rain had stopped during the night, but the ground was still wet. The trees were all black. She gave me a kiss. "Plant me one here," she said, touching her cheek. It was like any normal day, except my back was stiff and a little sore. I walked to the bus stop, and when she drove past, she honked the horn.

7. Hugged

I told all my friends about the mugging. They gathered around me. They touched my back. They wanted to see the cut. "Oohh," they moaned, and they hugged me and made me tell the story again.

"It's the worst thing that ever happened to me," I said. I must have said it half a dozen times that day. It was such a dramatic thing to say, but I meant it, too. It felt true. The worst thing. Not losing my jacket, not even being cut, but being helpless, at the mercy of someone else.

There was no way I could know that, within weeks, everything would change. I would think about the mugging quite differently, and in fact I would hardly remember it. What I would remember would be Mom and me sitting on the bed together, holding each other.

8. Mugged

They did a biopsy on the "freckle" on Mom's thigh. It was benign, but the doctor noticed that her spleen was swollen, and he did some tests. And then some more tests, and then he put her into the hospital for exploratory surgery. When they opened her up, they told me, they found cancer everywhere.

I live with Leo and Pepper now. They're good to me. I try not to think too much about Mom and the trailer and our life there. I notice that it makes people unhappy to see you unhappy, and they want to fix you up and tell you that everything will be all right. I can usually keep myself steady by listening to Mom. She's still giving me advice. *Sweetie pie, don't take it personally. One way or another, eventually we're all mugged by life.*

That was what she didn't want to say. She'd known it all along, but she didn't want me to know it—not yet, not this soon. She just wanted me to know enough so I'd be safe. I remember how she said life was like a river. You get pitched into it, and you don't get to choose where, deep waters or shallow, fast or calm.

She didn't want me to sink in that river. She, herself, swam all the time, until she couldn't anymore. She swam as hard as she could. She threw her arms around and kicked and kept her chin above water, and I expect I will, too.

Norma Fox Mazer on censorship

Some years ago, in a small town in Vermont, two seventh-grade girls picked up a book from their teacher's desk. One girl took it home. Her mother glanced through it and, alarmed, called the mother of the other girl. The book, *Saturday, the Twelfth of October*, had received excellent reviews, the Lewis Carroll Shelf Award, and was short-listed for the California Young Readers Medal. The parents cared not a fig for that stuff. Although they admitted that they had not read the book, they said they found themselves "grossly shocked and upset" by it.

It had disturbed other people, too, including the reviewer in the *New York Times*, who called the book "superb" but metaphorically wrung her hands over what she deemed excessive attention to things physical, such as menstruation, a complaint I found somewhat whimsical considering that it's a story of Stone Age people in a matriarchal society, in which the onset of the menarche is joyfully celebrated.

The Vermont parents called the police complaining about the use of such words as *piss, penis,* and *snot.* The police chief, himself, photocopied the offending pages; in effect, arrested the book. The mothers filed a formal complaint, using descriptive words and phrases such as "obscene ... sickening ... profanity ... loathsome impression ... perverted views ... turned my stomach ... foolish ... junk reading." All this and then the book was sent to the attorney general, who did read it and ruled that it had "serious literary value ... thus not a violation of ... the infamous obscenity statute. ... I trust," he added, "that none of the complainants have read Shakespeare, Chaucer, Salinger, Mailer, Updike, Cheever, Twain, Faulkner, and Hemingway, to name a few."

The brouhaha continued. The Board of Education met, the teacher was put on the spot, kids defended their right to choose their own reading, articles were written, and finally a restless peace was bought with a Board ruling that the book would be removed from the classroom.

This was my introduction to censorship. Now, after so many other battles, all of it sounds wearily familiar. I used to get a laugh out of the idea of my book being arrested. No more. Has censorship affected me, otherwise? I fervently hope not.

Still, where once I went to my writing without a backward glance, now I sometimes have to consciously clear my mind of those shadowy censorious presences. That's bad for me as a writer, bad for you as a reader. Censorship is crippling, negating, stifling. It should be unthinkable in a country like ours. Readers deserve to pick their own books. Writers need the freedom of their minds. That's all we writers have, anyway; our minds and imaginations. To allow the censors even the tiniest space in there with us can only lead to dullness, imitation, and mediocrity.

Spear turned around and flashed that sweet smile but Monroe didn't smile back and Janet's hard glare of hurt and fury killed any possibility of their budding relationship blooming into anything. Suddenly he was angry with her and with Monroe. Why couldn't they understand? He couldn't let Norma sit by herself. That was what white kids had done to his father in high school.

Spear

by
Julius Lester

"Spear! My man!"

"What's up, Spear! Didn't know you were in this class."

"Look out! Spear got a lock on all the *A*'s and he ain't even sat down yet."

The tall boy with skin the color of fallen oak leaves smiled shyly as he sauntered into the classroom.

"Hey, what's up, Jerome?" he said, pointing to a heavy-set dark-skinned boy in the back row. "You the man, Rocket," he continued, nodding to a boy in a Buffalo Bills football team T-shirt. Quickly, easily, he greeted everyone in the classroom like the natural politician he was.

Only after he sat down next to Janet (kissing her lightly on the cheek to the accompaniment of loud howls), did he notice the white girl sitting in the middle of the first row, two rows of empty desks between her and the rest of the class. Spear looked around at the brothers and sisters and raised his eyebrows. "This is African-American lit, right?" he asked no one in particular, though everyone, including the lone white girl, knew he was talking to her.

"That's what it says on my schedule," Janet chimed in. "Last period. *African*-American Literature."

Spear nodded. "That's what I thought."

"Hey, you! White girl!" Janet continued. "You sure you in the right class?"

Sitting next to the window Spear had a good look at her profile and that was enough for him to see how ordinary looking she was with dark blond hair cut to just above her shoulders, small eyes, a roundish face, lips as thin as a razor blade, and all of it packaged in a drab dark blue dress with yellow flowers. His father would've called her a skinny, ugly white bitch and that would have been that.

However, Spear was surprised when she turned and looked directly at him. Her chin was trembling and her voice shook as she said, "Well, y'all get to learn about all the white people what wrote books. How come I can't learn about all your people what wrote books?" And she turned back to staring at her desktop.

There was an embarrassed silence in the room. Janet frowned, her hostility not knowing where to go. "What's your name?" she asked sharply.

"Norma. Norma Jean Ray." Although her head was down and her back was to them, Spear could tell that she was ready to cry.

"You ain't no kin to James Earl Ray, are you?" a voice asked sarcastically, referring to the assassin of Martin Luther King, Jr. It was Monroe, his best friend.

"Chill!" Spear was startled to hear his voice, surprised by its loud command and the sudden and inexplicable mixture of anger and sadness he was feeling.

"What's your problem?" Monroe shot back. "I can't ask the girl a question?"

"Leave her alone," Spear responded.

"Excuse me!" Janet said, her unspent anger honing in on him

like a heat-seeking missile. "If you so afraid of Norma Jean *Whitey* getting her little *white* feelings hurt, maybe you better go sit next to her."

"Yeah! Maybe I should," he shot back, angry at the girl for having looked at him like that, though he could not say what "like that" was.

"Oh, oh," Monroe started. "Don't tell me my man Spear is coming down with a case of white-girl fever?"

Fortunately, the teacher walked in and Spear did not have to find out what he would have said or done—if anything. But throughout the class hour he caught himself looking covertly at the girl who seemed as if she had discovered the entire universe in her desktop.

* * *

"Spear" was not his real name but it was the only one he had ever heard. His father had been "Black Spear," the fiery black leader whose antiwhite speeches had caused race riots back in the seventies. He had been in his fifties when he married a young, regal, and very beautiful woman he renamed "Mother Eve" in honor of that first woman, an African, he claimed, from whom all humanity had come. When Mother Eve presented him with a son a year later, blacks hailed the child as his father's heir and called him "Little Spear." His parents had given him a more conventional name, that of her father, but even they never used it. After Black Spear's death his mother shortened his son's name to Spear. One day someone would preface the noun with an adjective.

He didn't like to think about that. Right now he just wanted to finish his last year of high school. He was class president as he had been his junior and sophomore years. Nobody had ever bothered to run against him, certainly nobody white, not in a school that was 75 percent black. But the white students liked Spear, too, and if not for him, more than one racial misunderstanding over the past three years might have turned in to something worse. Spear wondered sometimes what his father would have thought of his son being known more for stopping potential riots than starting them.

Almost every day he stayed late after school to tend to class business, or meet with the principal, class advisors, or yearbook editors, and generally didn't leave until five when the janitors locked up. He had just turned onto the main corridor when he saw her about to go out the front doors.

"Norma!" he called without thinking, sorry he had done so the instant he heard his voice reverberating with her name through the empty hallways.

She recognized the voice before she stopped and turned. "Hi," she greeted him nervously as he came up to her.

"Hi." Seeing her up close she really was about as attractive as a bowl of soggy cereal. Why had he called out as if he was glad to see her? And why did he suddenly find himself groping for something to say, he who always knew what to say?

They stood for a moment smiling awkwardly, as if one were a native and the other a tourist, but neither spoke the other's language. "What—what're you doing here so late?" he finally asked.

"Studying in the library."

"Oh." He nodded. "Are you new this year?"

She smiled ruefully and shook her head. "No. I've been here all the while. Since seventh grade."

"No!" he exclaimed, embarrassed.

"I'm used to it. There ain't no reason why anybody should notice me. Well, I got to go. The bus to Milltown comes at five-ten."

Milltown was where those whites lived who could not afford to move to the suburbs, where there were places with names like Croton and Pleasant Valley, when blacks began moving in ten years ago.

"If I miss it the next one ain't til six and I won't get home til six-thirty or so and it'll be hard to get supper ready by the time my daddy gets home around eight or nine." She laughed nervously. "My mama, she works third shift, from midnight to eight in the morning, and she's generally napping at supper time."

He started to offer her a ride but stopped. "Well, see you tomorrow. And, hey, I'm sorry about—about things I said before class started and about how Janet and Monroe treated you. They didn't mean anything by it."

Norma looked up at him and he felt ashamed as he had when she had looked at him in class. "Yes, they did," she said. There was no bitterness, anger, or even hurt in her voice. Just the flat tone of a truth he would have preferred to avoid. She ran out the door, down the steps, and toward the bus stop at the corner.

The next day when Spear walked into class she was already there in the middle seat of the front row. He responded perfunctorily to the shouted greetings from the back of the room and then hesitantly sat down beside her. The room was immediately silent. Spear didn't look at Norma but sensed her body stiffen as if wondering if he was making fun of her. That was not his intent, but why was he sitting there? All he knew was that when he walked in and saw her sitting alone again, it reminded him of something, but he didn't know what.

"Janet say if you don't get your black ass back here in a seat next to her, you best erase her phone number from your memory," Monroe said very loudly.

Spear turned around and flashed that sweet smile but Monroe didn't smile back and Janet's hard glare of hurt and fury killed any possibility of their budding relationship blooming into anything. Suddenly he was angry with her and with Monroe. Why couldn't they understand? He couldn't let Norma sit by herself. That was what white kids had done to his father in high school.

That was it! That was what she reminded him of. He didn't know if it was on one of the many videotaped interviews with his father or in his father's autobiography. "Those crackers couldn't keep me from going to the school but they didn't have to talk to me. From ninth grade all the way through high school I sat every day in every class in the front row, dead center, and the seats to my right were empty and the seats to my left were empty and the row behind me was empty and the row behind it was empty like I had leprosy or tuberculosis. All I had was a case of blackness. Not one of those honkies ever sat beside me or even called me by name. And the white man wonders why I want to wipe him off the face of the earth!"

That afternoon when he got home Spear went into the den where the videotapes of his father's speeches and interviews took up an entire wall. He had looked at all of them but one. Sometimes late at night he came downstairs and watched a speech of his father's, studying his walk, gestures, voice inflections. He found the tape on which his father told the story of his high school years and was pleased to see that he had remembered it correctly.

His mother came in from her office at the back of the house

where she worked writing articles and lectures to keep the image and ideas of Black Spear in people's minds and hearts until his son was ready to assume the mantle.

"Spear?" she called tentatively, looking at him staring at the blank television screen.

"Oh, hi," he said, getting up from the couch. "Mother," he continued abruptly, "if it was wrong when white kids made Daddy sit in class by himself all through high school, wouldn't it be wrong if black kids made a white student sit by himself?"

"Spear? What're you talking about?"

"Nothing. I was just curious." His voice went higher than he wished.

"Well, your father would say that no white person is alone because it's a white country. They're the majority. He would say it might be good for that white kid to sit there and feel isolated. Then he would know what blacks felt like every hour of every day."

"But wouldn't that white kid sitting in class alone surrounded by black kids hurt just as much as Daddy did being the only black surrounded by whites who wouldn't speak to him?"

These were not the kinds of questions Mother Eve wanted to hear from him.

Then he asked, "What—what would Daddy have thought if I went out with a white girl?" and she knew.

"Your father would've killed you before he let you do something like that," she responded without hesitating and without a smile.

Spear laughed nervously. "That's what I figured. Well, he's not here. So, what would you think?"

"Have you fallen in love with some white girl?" she asked sharply.

"No, Mama. I-I-I'm just curious. That's all." He tried to hide his nervousness by smiling but his mother did not smile back.

"And what would make you curious about pasty-faced white girls? With all the beautiful and intelligent black girls there are at that school and in this world, there is no reason why you or any black man has to go chasing after white women. And that goes double for the son of Black Spear!"

The next day he sat next to her in class again and afterward walked her to the school library. "Thanks for sitting next to me in class but you don't have to. I'm fine," she told him.

"I know," he responded.

He finished his student council meeting quickly and hurried to the library. She was sitting at a back table studying Afro-American lit. Having grown up in a household with more books of Afro-American history and literature than most libraries, the course was an easy A for him. It was all new to Norma Jean and he envied her the joy of discovery as she listened with intent interest as he answered her questions about Phyllis Wheatley, David Walker, and Frederick Douglass.

"What should I call you?" she asked as they walked to her locker where she put away her Afro-American lit book.

"Everybody calls me Spear."

"I can't call you that. It don't sound right coming from me. And, it don't feel like anybody I know."

"What do you mean?" His voice couldn't hide his eagerness for her answer.

"I don't know. I been practicing calling you Spear in my mind, but I don't know who I'm talking to."

She closed her locker and they walked in silence down the hallway and out the front door.

"Adrian," he said quietly. Though it was the name on official documents—his driver's license, bank account, school records—he had never said it aloud. Now that he had, it was as if he was giving her his soul.

He offered her a ride home. She shook her head. "My parents would want to kill me if they even heard I was in a car with somebody black."

She spent less and less time in the library after school and his meetings became shorter and shorter so they had more time to sit in an empty classroom and talk or walk to the far end of the soccer field and sit with their backs against a large oak tree and talk some more. What they said was not as important as their learning how words can measure the beat of another's heart, and one afternoon he looked at her and was startled to see that she was really quite beautiful.

* * *

Three weeks passed and one morning Spear drove into the school parking lot and found Monroe waiting for him.

"We got to talk," Monroe began as Spear got out of his car. He had stayed at Monroe's when his parents were on the road and for longer periods after his father died.

"Something happen?" Spear asked anxiously. "Somebody die or something?"

"Don't you know? If you don't, then things are more serious than I thought."

"You want to speak English, homes?" Spear asked, getting exasperated.

"Some of the brothers and sisters asked me to talk to you about that white girl. Even your mother has been calling my house almost every night wanting me to tell her what you're doing, who the girl is, and begging me to talk some sense into you."

"Damn!"

"I mean, come on, bro. If you've really come down with white-girl fever, it's understandable. There are some fine white bitches in this school and I would be more understanding if you tried to get over your fever with somebody like Angie O'Connor or Jennifer Turner, somebody with bigger tits than a three-year-old and an ass with more meat on it than a dog that hasn't eaten for a week."

"What's it to you?" Spear responded, his voice barely above a whisper, his body rigid.

"Whoa, bro. This is me, Monroe, your ace, talking to you. Have you forgotten who you are, man? You're our leader. Black people haven't had a real one since your father died. You can't let your people down. You understand. If this was a sex thing, you know, I don't think anybody would be upset, except some of the sisters, and even they understand that a brother might have to take a dip in a blond, brunette, or redhead pool from time to time." He laughed. "But you're hung up on this white girl, Spear, and that ain't good."

Spear didn't go to the Afro-Am lit class that day. Instead he went home and there, from the very top shelf, he took down the tape he had never looked at. The thirteen-year-old images flickered on the screen to show a five-year-old boy holding his father's hand as they walk along a school corridor where his father has just given a speech. People are pushing to get close to his father. His father reaches down to pick him up so that he will be above the crowd. Just as he does, a white man holding a pistol comes into view. His father does not see the man. Neither does the boy. They are looking at each other, smiling. Then just as his father puts his hands beneath Little Spear's arms, the man pulls the trigger. Once, twice. Both bullets tear into his father's side, the force spinning him onto his back. Instead of the hands lifting the boy they drag him down and Little Spear stumbles, falling across his father's bleeding body.

Spear gasped and tears came to his eyes but then, he thought he noticed something. Wiping at his eyes he rewound the videotape. His father has just been shot and Spear has fallen across his body. There! The white man starts to pull the trigger for a third shot but stops. Spear rewound the tape again and this time advanced it in slow motion. His father falls onto his back, Spear falls across him, the man starts to fire again but doesn't. No one is close enough to stop him. It is also clear that Black Spear is still alive. Yet, the man lowers the pistol and waits calmly for the police.

Spear rushed to the back of the house to his mother's study. "Mama. I want you to look at something," he implored her.

When she saw what tape it was, she didn't want to look.

"I know it's hard, Mama, but please look. It's important!" He pressed the play button and the tape advanced. When the white man appeared Spear slowed the tape. "Watch." When the tape ended he asked, "Did you see it? Did you see it?"

"See what, Spear? What has gotten into you lately?"

"Please watch the man with the gun. Watch carefully."

He rewound the tape and played it again. "There. Right there! Daddy's down. Look at the man's finger on the trigger. He is about to shoot again. But look! His finger relaxes."

His mother was getting annoyed. "So he didn't shoot again. He could see your father was dead. The police were coming. He got scared. How do I know why that honky didn't kill you, too?"

Spear shook his head. "Daddy didn't die for another day, did he? It was at least another minute before the police outside made it through the crowd. And the man wasn't scared because he waited for the police."

"I give up," her voice scarcely able to hide the sarcasm. "Why didn't he kill you?"

"You always told me that the man who killed Daddy hated black people. But I was lying on top of Daddy. He should've killed me because I could grow up and have twenty black children."

"What's your point, Spear?"

"The man who killed my father didn't hate black people. He just hated Daddy."

His mother slapped him hard, once, twice, across the face.

Tears came to Spear's eyes but not as much from the slaps. "You might as well hit me again, Mama. I think I'm in love with a white girl." His voice was low and steady.

The next afternoon as he left class with Norma, he said, "I-I need to talk to you about something, need to ask you something." They walked to the tree beside the soccer field and sat down.

"Would you go out with me?" he blurted without prelude.

Norma laughed nervously. "Have you lost your mind?"

This was not the response he had expected. "What—what do you mean?"

"You could have any girl in this school. What do you want with me? Adrian, I'm a nobody. I'm not pretty. I'm not real smart. My folks are racist *and* poor. You've been real nice to me and I appreciate it, but you don't have to go this far."

"I know that," he said, almost angrily. "And I don't feel sorry for you. I like you and I want to go out with you."

"Why? Nobody has ever asked me out. Now, all of a sudden, I'm supposed to believe that the most famous and best-looking boy in school wants to go out with little Norma Jean Ray, little *white* Norma Jean Ray? It don't make sense."

"It does to me. You asked me my name. Nobody ever asked me to be myself. When I talk to you I feel different. All my life, no matter what I did, I would wonder what my father would think, what he would say. But now I care about what you think of me. And yesterday I did something and for the first time, I guess, I really understood. My father's dead. What's important is what *I* think of me."

"I'm flattered. I really am, but what about your people? I see how they look up to you. And I see how hurt they are by our being together so much. They need you."

"They needed my father, too. I needed my father. I guess my father needed them more than he needed me. Well, I don't think *I* need them. I don't want to be their spear."

The phone rang late that night while he was watching a videotape of one of his father's speeches, but with the sound off. His mother had gone to bed. The two of them had not spoken since the previous afternoon.

"Hello."

"Adrian?" the voice at the other end whispered.

"Hi," he responded softly, smiling in a way he never had.

"I hope it's OK I called so late. I wanted to call before but my mom and dad and I had a big fight tonight."

"What did you fight about?"

"That's partly why I'm calling. What—what you said to me this afternoon was beautiful. It made me feel real special. I've never been special to anybody before. I've thought a lot about what you said, about us going out together and all."

"And?"

"I'm sorry, Adrian. I'm sorry. I'm not brave like you. You don't seem to notice how kids stare at us in school. All the black girls want to rip my hair out of my skull and the white boys want to beat me up. I wish I was brave like you, but I'm not. And, anyway, once you got to *really* know me, you'd be wondering what you thought you saw in me." She laughed nervously. "I guess it hurts less this way. I can say no and you'll keep on thinking that I'm this wonderful person. And it doesn't matter anyway since I won't be coming to school anymore."

"What're you talking about?"

"Well, the reason I stayed after school to study African-American Literature and left my book in my locker was so my parents wouldn't find out. I knew they would go through the roof if they found out. Well, somebody told them about me taking the class and also about me and you." She stopped and when she resumed her voice had the same tremble as it had the first time she looked at him. "There's a school run by one of the churches, an all-white school, and that's where I'll be going starting Monday."

"Are you serious? They can't do that!"

"They already have. I got to go. You've given me the happiest moments of my entire life. Adrian?"

"Yes."

"I love you."

And before he could respond, she hung up.

It was a while before everyone at school stopped calling him Spear and called him Adrian, as he requested. They were surprised when he resigned as class president. He seemed sadder and yet happier. He was just Adrian now and it wasn't long before people wondered why they had ever thought he was extraordinary and he became almost as anonymous as she had been.

Adrian and his mother seldom spoke. This was supposed to have been the year he would travel with her on speaking engagements and she could introduce him to the people he needed to know and let him try out a few speeches of his own. "That's not what I want to do with my life," he told her.

So he stayed in his room and played games on his computer, and spent hours on the World Wide Web marveling at how big the world was.

Once a week or so, late at night, his phone rang. He always answered before the first ring stopped.

"Hello."

"Adrian?"

"Hi."

"It's me."

"I know."

She couldn't talk for fear of being overheard, but at least she was there. So he talked about what was going on at school, not that he paid much attention anymore, what they were reading in African-American Literature class, and what videos he had rented, the only kind he watched now. Mostly, though, he said nothing, and neither knew that each held the receiver so tightly that their hands hurt.

Sometimes the silence was like a gulf that could never be crossed. Most of the time, though, the gulf only opened when she said, "Good night, Adrian. I love you," and he heard the phone go dead.

----

on censorship

Those who would censor books fear what I fear—a loss of control. Therein lies the extraordinary power of the word. Language can seduce us into forgetting where we are and who we are; it can make us believe in things we know rationally could never be; it can resurrect experiences of pain, discomfort, and suffering we thought we had forgotten. Is it any wonder that Plato banned poets from his utopia?

Sometimes it is difficult to write knowing there are forces waiting to seize upon what they consider to be an "objectionable" word, scene, or character in something I've written. Sometimes it is difficult not to censor myself and not write a particular scene because of the anticipated fight with an editor or publisher who's worried that sales might be affected adversely.

So, I remind myself that my ultimate obligation is to the realm of the imagination and give voice to the infinite stories residing in the human spirit. Those who seek to have power over what I write violate something fundamental to a democratic society. That is the quality of trust.

Perhaps nothing is so wounding to a writer than being accused of having written something that hurts a child. Censorship is an attitude of mistrust and suspicion that seeks to deprive the human experience of mystery and complexity. But without mystery and complexity there is no wonder; there is no awe; there is no laughter.

So, yes, there are times when I write something and am afraid that this one might "get me in trouble" again. But what is the alternative? To write and not tell the truth? That would be death for any writer. But more, it would be death to the imagination. And if the imagination dies, what will happen to the souls of children?

It occurred to me that if I were someone else I would've been crammed into a stall with another girl, my best friend, telling her what had happened, sharing every detail and making it feel more real, more important, more special somehow. I've watched girls caucus about their boyfriends, do you think he likes me what does it mean that he looked at me that way why didn't he say hello. *I'm just not the romance-and-intrigue type. I'm five-ten, allergic to makeup, and can bench one-and-a-half times my weight. It'd be hard to pull off acting girlic.*

Going Sentimental

by
Rachel Vail

"I have to call Aunt Tillie," I said. As soon as the words were out I closed my eyes.

"What?" Mackey asked, out of breath on top of me.

"Nothing," I whispered, trying to refocus on losing my virginity. With my eyes squeezed shut, all I could see was Aunt Tillie's face, which didn't help.

My mind had wandered. It started with thinking, *Oh my god, I'm losing my virginity.* Then since I didn't know what more to think about that, I thought, *Well, when I'm done I have to let the dog back in and make sure the footprints are wiped off the foyer floor so my mother won't know we've been here, cutting school and losing our virginity.* That led to realizing I should remember the date, because this is an Important Milestone. And then I remembered that the date is January 14—Aunt Tillie's birthday, she's turning eighty today—and out it fell from my mouth, "I have to call Aunt Tillie!" My one utterance during the loss of my virginity. No "I love you." Just "Aunt Tillie."

Figures.

By the time I finished reviewing my space-out, we were done. Mackey lay beside me on the playroom floor, and the sheet he had spread beneath us was crumpled over near the Ping-Pong table. My back felt sandpapered from the indoor-outdoor carpeting my parents had industriously put down themselves one weekend last year. They live for home improvements. My parents. Oh, god. Busy, rolled-sleeve Lutherans who would never tolerate a mess or doubt my virginity. Which reminded me, I had to remember to fold the sheet.

I almost popped right up to do it but instead I looked over at Mackey first. He was blinking sleepily, one arm resting on his forehead, his other arm under my neck. His naked hairless chest is probably as familiar to me as my own. We've been best friends since fifth grade and a couple since seventh. People are shocked we've waited this long, but I felt like we should at least have our driver's licenses. Mackey protested, "They don't check," but he was joking, not pressuring. He may have a neck as thick as my waist and a stomach so hard you can stand on it, but inside he's a total softie. Anyway, I got my license a month ago. We've both been taking deep breaths with eyebrows raised and shrugging at each other since then. Our chemistry teacher was absent today which meant we'd have to spend the period in study hall staring at the walls. He looked at me with his gray eyes wide and pleading. I said, "Good a time as any."

He yelled, "Much!" and did a little dance in the hall. I grabbed him by the jacket before we could get detention and dragged him out to my car. We couldn't find anything good on the radio on the way to my house, so we listened to the traffic report. We decided that would be our song.

He's the one who thought of the sheet, which he spread out gently across the playroom rug. He stood in the center of it and said, "C'mere." Then we did it.

"You OK?" he asked me, pulling my face toward his.

"Mm-hmm." I kissed him on his warm rough cheek with my eyes closed. My hair flopped into my mouth.

He lifted my hair and tucked it behind my ear, and whispered, "You were really into it, huh?"

"No, yeah, it was fine." I stood up and pulled my underwear out of my sweatpants. "We should fold the sheet."

"In all those sex stories in *Penthouse,*" Mackey said, up on his elbow, watching me struggle into my clothes, "the women never moan, 'I have to call Aunt Tillie.' "

"I'm sorry; it's her birthday," I said, trying to maintain my balance while pulling on socks standing up. As long as we've been together I still can't get normal when I'm naked and he's watching. "Come on. We gotta go."

He sat up to fiddle with the condom. I turned around and yanked my sports bra over my head. Not to be immature but he could've gone to the bathroom.

I heard him stand up and walk over to me but I didn't turn toward him. "Do you want to go get a, something?" he asked, wrapping his arms around my waist. "A coffee? A cigarette?"

I shrugged him off me. Neither of us has ever tried coffee or cigarettes. We're both athletes and, besides, his father died of a heart attack at forty, probably because he smoked. Obviously Mackey didn't mean *literally.* I got the reference. It just pissed me off anyway. "Mackey," I said. He was still naked.

"Now, she murmurs my name," he complained, heading for the bathroom. While he was gone, I grabbed my basketball shirt from on top of his half-inside-out sweatshirt. I pulled it on, then flipped my head over and gathered my hair into a ponytail. That's that, I told myself. Got rid of it. No big deal. Fold the sheet.

I was up in the kitchen by the time Mackey had finished in

the downstairs bathroom, and he wandered up to find me. He looked a little bewildered, holding his green-striped tube socks loosely in his fist. I forced myself to flash him a quick smile as I closed the back door behind the dog.

He smiled back. He grinned, actually. I shook my head, but felt myself smiling in return. I can never help it, when he gets that look on his face, so pleased with himself and me and life in general. I reached into the cabinet to get the dog a treat, to bribe her for her silence. The only witness to what we'd done. Sort of witness. There's no window in the playroom so she didn't actually watch or anything.

With my face deep in the cabinet I said, "That wasn't so bad, huh?" My hands were shaking a little on the box of biscuits.

"Oh, great," Mackey answered. "Not so bad. I'm new at this, too, you know."

"No," I protested. I gripped two Snausages in my fist and squeezed. "I meant . . ."

"I know what you meant, you crank," he said, balancing on one foot to pull on his sock. "Me, too."

I didn't want to get into a whole thing so I pushed past him without making eye contact to give the dog her treats.

"What's your rush?" Mackey asked, trying to catch hold of my face as I went by him.

I turned on the kitchen faucet to wash my hands. "I have a game," I said.

"But . . ."

"Come on, Mackey. Let's go." I picked up my keys and wet a paper towel. He followed me to the foyer and sat beside me on the mat, as we always do to put on our shoes. His red high-tops are size thirteen wide. We really do know everything about each other. He uses only green pens. He worries how he'll pay for college and that his nose is too big. His locker combination is 13-2-22. I backed toward the door, using the wet paper towel to wipe our footprints off the white tiles. He held the door open for me. I locked up. In movies there's more, well, something. Sweat. Background music. Staring. They don't have to pull their underwear off their sweat-pants, after, and drive a rusting Toyota over to the high school gym.

Mackey turned on the radio while we were stopped at a light. "See if you can find the traffic," I said.

He laughed, but then I guess I hit the gas too hard when the light changed. He was still looking for a station so he got flung back against his seat. He turned the radio off and watched the houses out the window.

While I was pulling into a parking spot, Mackey whispered, "Do you feel different?"

"About you?" I yanked up the emergency brake.

"Yeah. Or yourself? Or us?"

He leaned across the gear shift to force me to look at him. He's lucky he's so hugely muscular because his mouth is very pretty, almost girlie, the way the lips are so red and almost pursed, and his soft gray eyes that lock on me like there's nobody else.

"You're not going sentimental on me, are you?" I asked.

"Damn," he said. "You really have no appreciation of how smooth I am at all, do you?" He smiled and tried to kiss me. I let my lips brush his, then turned off the ignition and flung open my door. He ran after me. "It didn't hurt, did it, Jody?" he whispered.

"No," I said.

"Promise?" He rested his heavy arm on my shoulder.

"I have to get to the gym." I checked my watch. I was early and he knew it.

"OK," he said. He slowed down or maybe I sped up, and I didn't look back.

In the locker room I dialed my combination and carefully pulled out my basketball shorts and high-tops, which I set neatly on the bench. I closed my locker and sank down against it, resting my forehead on my knees.

Well, that's done, I told myself. In a totally responsible way, with someone I've been going out with for four years, in the middle of the afternoon, in the safety of my home. No big deal.

No big deal.

So, good.

By the time I lifted my head, some of my teammates had come in, and there was the usual ruckus of getting ready for a game. The visiting team sucked so we were feeling pretty cocky. Still, by game time we were all focused, concentrating, our hair pulled back tight, our laces double-bowed. I hadn't said a word to anyone about the afternoon. Just "Hey" a few times, to teammates getting ready near me. "What's up." That's about the extent of it.

Mackey is my best friend, always has been, so I've avoided the whole girl-politics thing. It occurred to me that if I were someone else I would've been crammed into a stall with another girl, my best friend, telling her what had happened, sharing every detail and making it feel more real, more important, more special somehow. I've watched girls caucus about their boyfriends, *do you think he likes me what does it mean that he looked at me that way why didn't he say hello.* I'm just not the romance-and-intrigue type. I'm five-ten, allergic to makeup, and can bench one-and-a-half times my weight. It'd be hard to pull off acting girlie.

During the pep talk, while Coach was reminding us *Get back on defense,* I scanned the faces around me. I could trust any of them to be where she should be to receive a no-look pass. That's about it. Which of them could I imagine gripping by the arms and whispering with wide eyes how it had felt, this afternoon? No, not one of them. Well, I'm a very private person and some things are nobody's business but my own.

Like, What does it mean if you feel just nothing much, after?

I was a little sore, actually, I realized, down there. I walked out with the team into the white lights and echoes of the gym. Get back on defense. Don't start in on *maybe it's not true love.* True Love. What did I expect? Like, a symphony? Flowers? Slow motion? It's just me and Mackey. JodyandMackey, one word. Maybe if you've been going out forever, there's not that much romance left. Maybe that's why people do it with a fling—maybe there's more passion.

Passion. Not a word I've ever once in my life said out loud. I'm a jock, for god's sake. What do I want with passion? Romance. That's for girls who rush home after school to pant over their soaps.

I low-fived my teammates when my name was called, and crouched to wait with the other starters for the opening whistle. The ball thumped into my palm, its hard nubbiness solid and reassuring. I dribbled twice and hit an open teammate, and she sunk a quick layup to put us up two points before the other team had touched the ball. "Yes," a few of us huffed, slapping one another's butts, ready to bury the suckers.

I shuffled backward on defense, in the rhythm of the game now, sneakers squeaking, hands up, breath coming fast but regular. No way was this girl getting past me. I was so on her, so sure of myself, I had time to flick my eyes up to the stands.

I stopped center court when I saw him. The girl I'd been

guarding so tight crashed into me and fell on her butt. The ball rolled toward the sidelines, but I didn't budge, didn't grab it to make the easy put-in. My teammates were screaming my name but I just rested my hands on my hips and smiled up at Mackey who was grinning triumphantly down at me. He was standing alone, his size-thirteen-wide red high-tops spread far apart, on the top row of the bleachers. His arms were straight up, clutching a sign made out of oak tag he'd obviously yanked off the wall behind him, where there was a gap in the line of school-spirit posters.

In giant green letters he'd scrawled: HAPPY BIRTHDAY AUNT TILLIE.

Rachel Vail on censorship

The first time I visited a school, the principal pulled me aside and confided that she hadn't read my book, and needed to ask me if there were "any bad words in it." I assured her that I tried to choose only good words.

But I had made a vow to myself when I was a teenager that I would never forget, and never disrespect, the intensity of the adolescent experience, the power and terror of being a person actively creating herself. Some of the choices teenagers make are morally and practically wrong. Some of my characters do things I hope my child won't. There are occasionally words my characters choose that I wouldn't utter in my mother's presence. But when I was sixteen, or twelve, hanging out with my friends? That was different. For a story to feel real, I have to respect what a character would really do or say.

I believe in any person's right to read whatever she or he chooses. It astonishes me that there are people who believe that by simply avoiding a discussion of sex, for instance, or cruelty, that they can protect the children in their community from any experience of these things. When I receive censorious letters about something I've written, I write back commending the involvement and passion but asking the concerned adult if she or he might be able to use the offensive situation as a platform for discussion—*Do you think this character did the right thing? What other possibilities existed for her?* I've actually never heard back so I don't know if a discussion has followed. I hope so. What more can I do?

I can get back to work. Today, as everyday, I'll sit at my desk trying to become the character I'm creating, asking myself questions: Who am I? What do I want? What am I willing to risk, to get it? Who is stopping me, and why, and how? I'll try to find the most compelling action, a true and difficult crisis, honest thoughts, real consequences. The paths this character and I chose today might end up offending somebody, maybe even me. But that's not what matters, so I'll push that consideration aside. I'll just try, again and again, to choose good words.

I can hear, even now, the pulsing of the drums as through the rice fields I walked and ran down the narrow path until my breath came hard, so that I unbuttoned the top of my school uniform. I was young, and obsessed, I suppose, for who could call my feeling "love" except another green boy like myself. She was my teacher, and I had no right to hold toward her the feeling a man holds for a woman.

The Red Dragonfly

by
Katherine Paterson

On our island the last nights of August are swollen with the promise of typhoon. There is a beauty about them, but it cannot hide a restless stirring of a fear one seeks to hush with: "This is only the natural course of the world. Every summer it is so. It has always been so and will remain so while the world stands." But the fear persists. Perhaps that is why our fathers in ancient days chose this season for *Obon*, for one cannot help believe that the sultry air is indeed teeming with the spirits of the unknown—the dead which must be placated.

Yet it is not of the unknown dead that I would write, but of the living, who though known to us, are still unknown. I would write of myself—the self I knew, yet did not know that August night when the chorus of cicadas and frogs was joined by the coarse cries of men celebrating the festival of the dead.

I can hear, even now, the pulsing of the drums as through the rice fields I walked and ran down the narrow path until my breath came hard, so that I unbuttoned the top of my school uniform. I was young, and obsessed, I suppose, for who could call my feeling "love" except another green boy like myself. She was my teacher, and I had no right to hold toward her the feeling a man holds for a woman.

I was ashamed, and often condemned myself for this foolishness. But even as my mind played the stern judge, the corners of
my heart would curl in a smile I could not prevent. In years, she
could not have been much my elder, and she had the way of
Japanese women who appear even younger than they are, with
skin like polished pine and shining eyes—so shining—shining
like the glint of a dragonfly's wing in the sunlight.

A dragonfly. It was her body, at once graceful and quick—the
movement of her slender hands. Some women are cats and some
foxes. I have seen women who were big-footed and patient like
the water buffalo at the plow, but she in her bright shining would
have made swallows appear as clumsy as these buffalo. And so,
though the memory still has power to catch and twist my belly
as I say it, she was like the red dragonfly of the late summer, del-
icate herald of autumn, precursor of the year's loveliness.

I had written a poem, a haiku. How well I remember the rush
of blood to my scalp, the hotness of my shaven student's head, as
the lines fell into the ancient pattern, breaking into newness by
my hand.

> *Tomoshibini*   On the lantern
> *Tomarite tombo*   Rests a dragonfly
> *Aki no tomo.*   Friends of autumn.

The lantern was, of course, the student's lamp on the low
desk before which I squatted each night, pounding, through a
head made thicker by the heat, interminable answers to end-
less possible questions. My father was determined that one of
his sons enter the university, and since I was physically weak-
est, he reasoned that I was mentally superior to my brothers.
So those two destined to be farmers were now among the
laughing and singing voices which punctuated my labored

memorizations. Except for me, the house was empty, as indeed all the houses in the village were that night. I was alone in the dim light wrestling with a proscribed destiny when I noticed the friend who had come to keep me company. It was a red dragonfly lighting on my lamp. My heart went out to the tiny creature and leapt from its quivering form to her whom in my heart I called a dragonfly. And in the foolishness of my youth I saw an omen.

* * *

Even in my haste, I took care to make ink and brush the lines onto the best paper we had. The lines raced through my pen onto the page before me, and before they were even dry on the page, I knew I would take them to her. Carefully I folded my poem into a second paper. The drums for dancing had begun in the center of the village, and the pulse in my temple rose to their same pitch as I stroked her name upon the outer fold. Hot as it was, I put the jacket of my uniform on and buttoned it formally to the throat. Foolishly I remember Raskolnikov preparing for his crime, as, despite my pounding pulse, I put away all evidence of my brush writing, taking care to replace the paper in just the slightly skewed fashion in which I had found it. I put out my lamp, and in the light of the festival moon, slipped into my clogs and made my way through the fields toward the sounds of revelry.

I walked, then ran, and as the nearing drums quickened the rhythm of my body beyond its accustomed beat, I was choking out each breath. When I came to the village, I rounded its edge, lest I be caught by the crowd of merrymakers or seen by my father. But by now I was fully entangled in the noise and imbued by it with a spirit not my own.

I would slip into the entranceway of her house and leave the poem on the platform there, I thought as I ran. But her mother . . . then I would wait. Her mother being old would doubtless come home earlier, and when her mother was in, then I would leave the poem for her to discover. I did not plan after that. For youth there is only the act. It consumes all time. We learn to be cautious for consequences later.

There was no light from her house. Like a criminal I looked furtively in all directions, then slid into a dark place between a large bush in the garden and the low wall which separated her house from the neighbor's. There I waited. My hand was over my mouth to muffle my pained breathing, as I crouched, my eyes straining for the path by which she would return.

The noise of *Obon* grew louder as the night grew old. Occasionally now a voice could be heard distinct from the festival din—the voice of the old taking reluctant children home. At last two women turned the corner and, talking loudly, as old women tend to on such a night, they paused in the street, their tired voices raised in countermelody to the wild, impatient music throbbing against my temple.

"Well then, sleep well." The one bobbed a familiar good night.

"Sleep well," responded the other.

I could hear the neighbor's clogs tock-tocking down the cobble street. The old one lingered a moment at the low gate as if loath to relinquish the night, but at length she turned down the path.

My body tightened further into itself, but I need not have feared. She looked to neither side, but went straight to her door, pushed it aside, slipped in, and shoved it back more loudly than a woman who knows she is being observed.

When at last the noises of quiet busyness came from the house, I crept to the entranceway. Suddenly afraid of the noise the door might make, I slid the poem through the crack and heard it fall on the earthen floor. Then I picked my way back through the shadows and bushes to my watching place.

The moon was past its zenith now. In the lengthening shadows my cramped body allowed itself the luxury of shifting and stretching. I was becoming used to my vigil and began to look about me with some little pleasure—to drink in that which I knew her to taste each day. The garden was small, but, to my unpracticed eye, tastefully arranged about a tiny fish pond. Near its edge was a stone lantern, not of remarkable age and style, but a comfortable guardian of the surroundings. The sliding doors of the room adjacent were still dark. The only light came from the north side of the house where her mother prepared for sleep. In my imagination her mother lay out a pallet for her, arranging the quilt and patting the husk pillow for her head to lie on. Thus I embroidered the details of her life in which she was a daughter and not a teacher, in which she looked to her mother as I to mine, until, suddenly, my dreams were punctured by a woman's laugh. She was coming. But a man's voice rose and fell in teasing syllables threaded by her laughter. She was not coming alone.

What could I do? It was too late to run, too late to retrieve the poem. I could only wait, sweat pouring down my body. The drums were fainter now, but my pulse remained captive to their beat.

He slammed the door aside. "What!" His voice exploded the syllable. "Ah, something for you." He was holding up my poem to read in the moonlight. "A love poem no doubt," he grunted amiably, handing it to her.

"No doubt." Her laughter shimmered in the night.

She followed him in, closing the door gently behind her. I could hear him mount the platform into the house. She paused to straighten both pairs of clogs and then followed him into the south room. The light went on. I saw her form moving across the room, preparing pallets for the night.

I would have left then. I rose to go, but a shaft of light falling on the stone lantern had caught a glint. I turned, hardly meaning to, and saw there on the lantern the hideous thing. It was a giant mantis on its haunches. In its not quite human limbs it grasped a dragonfly. The tiny wings glistened as the body quivered in the mantis's jaws. Hate flooded my body.

"Araaa!" I snatched off my right clog, raised it, and brought it down again and again and again to beat, beat, beat the evil creature.

"Who's there?" A man's voice called roughly from the house.

I dropped the clog and ran limping to the street. The gravel cut my bare foot as I ran—not home but toward the narrow bridge which spans the Yoshino. I stopped at the bank of the black river and kicked my left foot high into the air and listened several seconds for the faint splash far below.

Katherine Paterson on censorship

I try not to let incidents of challenge or censorship affect my writing. Self-censorship can be very damaging to a story. When our chief goal is not to offend someone, we are not likely to write a book that will deeply affect anyone. These days, however, with my work appearing with alarming frequency on the list of challenged books, I look more closely at certain words or paragraphs that I realize may cause trouble for teachers or librarians who use or recommend my books. It is very painful for me when someone else has to put her or his reputation or livelihood on the line because of something I have written. I try to make sure that any potentially troublesome parts of my work are absolutely necessary to the sense and power of what I am trying to say. I do not want to make life harder for the very people who are responsible for sharing my books with the young.

I know that when a book is challenged, I will not be the one who suffers. It will be the teacher or librarian who is called upon to defend what I have written who must stand in the line of fire. They are true heroes to me—the guardians of the constitutional freedoms which make this country great. I admire them more than I can say. If we lose their witness, we will have lost democracy itself.

Pretty soon, the fire's just smoke and people crying and the crowd starts moving away. With the fire and all, it's that kind of day makes you want to holler but Claytena's sitting there looking evil so I just sort of groan and leave it at that. I lift my T-shirt to my nose and smell the smoke settled in it. Everything around me is smoke and water and July heat.

July Saturday

by
Jacqueline Woodson

Me and Claytena Smalls are sitting on my fence watching the Williams' house go up in smoke. Chuck Williams comes running out with his mama's Maxwell House can, the one she keeps all her quarters in—her rainy day quarters. Chuck's crying and Ms. Williams's crying and my own mama is already over there, wrapping her arms around Ms. Williams and pulling the baby to her. Claytena's kind of watching the whole scene like she's a hundred miles away from it. She's got her eyes squinted up and her chin sitting on her fists. Every little while, the smoke gets so thick, the whole scene disappears, then the wind blows and it's right back in front of us. Claytena and Chuck were, just the night before, making out behind the handball courts, so it was almost certain that Chuck would have been asking her out today had his house not caught on fire. Claytena's pretty, prettier than me, with kind of red-brown skin and near-black eyes.

"Who's that lady?" she asks, lifting her head real quick.

There's a woman standing kind of off a ways from everybody else. She's tall and skinny, doesn't look familiar.

I shrug and go back to watching the house burn. Up on the top floor I can see firemen running back and forth between the windows. I see them go in where Chuck's room used to be and come out by the baby's. One of them tosses a handful of smoky clothing out the window but none of the Williamses move forward to grab it.

"Probably just somebody come to watch," I say. I see my mama's arm slide around the baby's shoulder and pull her in close. The baby's not really a baby, closer to four or five and capable of standing and walking and talking. I've seen her do plenty of all of it. Real name's Justine after Mr. Williams whose first name's Justin. Everybody calls her the baby though being she came so long after Chuck—some ten years—and for all those years in between Ms. Williams was talking about her wishes for a baby. I get a strange feeling watching Mama hold Justine. Kind of runs down my chest and just sort of flip-flops at the bottom of my stomach.

"She doesn't look like she's from around here," Claytena says.

In school, our teacher promised extra credit if we could name all fifty states in any kind of order. I got as far as California, counting one-Mississippi before each one as a means of an order. Teacher said putting one-Mississippi before something didn't give it any order even if I could name three states in a row that way. I took out the one-Mississippi and just named states but still could only come up with a few before I started stumbling. Claytena made it all the way through talking about Alabama, Arizona, California, Connecticut, and on and on, like she was born reciting the fifty states in A–B–C order.

I give the lady a good hard look. She's wearing a leather vest and got a leather knapsack kind of hanging from her shoulders. Every now and again, she shifts from one foot to the other but doesn't do much more than that. That and watching the fire. I look a little harder and see she's not really a lady, just a regular teenager—maybe seventeen or eighteen, but maybe younger, too. She's one of those teenagers with airs—holding her head up a bit like she's looking down on everything. Those kind of teenagers are the ones that make me can't wait to be one—so I can look down, too. See what they're seeing.

"You figure she bought that knapsack and vest as a set?" I say but Claytena just kind of rolls her eyes at me and then slides them back over to the teenager. After a while she gets up and I'm fearing she's going to go ask the teenager about her business. But she just kind of stands there with her arms folded, looking mean, then sits back down again.

Pretty soon, the fire's just smoke and people crying and the crowd starts moving away. With the fire and all, it's that kind of day makes you want to holler but Claytena's sitting there looking evil so I just sort of groan and leave it at that. I lift my T-shirt to my nose and smell the smoke settled in it. Everything around me is smoke and water and July heat.

There's never been a fire on this street but people don't seem too put out by it. Down the block, three little girls start untangling a double-Dutch rope and Mr. Wheeler, whose house sits right where our street starts to curve into the woods, is standing with his barbecuing apron still on, a spatula in his hand— like he doesn't really know what to do or say next. That's where we all were—at Mr. Wheeler's barbecue when the flames starting shooting out of the window. I had a burger, just about to take another bite out of it, and Chuck and Claytena were holding hands and walking off to the other side of Mr. Wheeler's pool. It was Justine who came running into the yard yelling that her baby doll was burning up. I watch the smoke rise up from the piles of clothes in the yard—everything seeming like it happened a long time ago.

"You ever get the feeling like your life just stops sometimes, Clay?"

Claytena looks at me for a minute. "I guess."

We get quiet. After a few minutes Claytena shrugs. "Then sometimes it feels like it's moving real fast—like some crazy ride I can't get off of."

"Centrifugal force," I say. "Like that ride that goes around so fast you stick to the walls."

"I hate that ride."

"Me, too."

Me and Claytena sit on that fence just staring up and down the street. After a while, I see Mama and Ms. Williams heading up toward us. Mama's got the baby up in her arms now and Ms. Williams is carrying the Maxwell House can like it's something fragile.

"You think this means the Williamses're going to be staying with us a while, Clay?"

Claytena shrugs then jumps down from the fence to go meet up with them. The baby's crying real soft and has her two fingers in her mouth. Claytena takes her from Mama and Mama wraps both arms around Ms. Williams. They make their way slowly up the block. I see Chuck running fast in the opposite direction and Mr. Williams leaning on somebody's car. He lights up a cigarette, takes a drag, throws it on the ground, then lights up another one.

I see the teenager watching him, shifting from foot to foot, just staring.

"Child, if you don't get up off that fence and get in there and start fixing something for us, you better."

"Yes, Mama." I climb over the fence into our front yard. Then all of us are heading into my house with me leading the way.

* * *

They have all kinds of names for this neighborhood. Used to be called "up and coming," trees lining the street real pretty and people keeping their properties nice. Somewhere along the way it switched to some kind of class—upper-working or lower-wealthy or something in between. By the time we got here it had pretty much settled into itself, somewhere between middle and upper depending on which side of the street you live on. Seems college professors had their side, buying up houses next door to small-timey lawyers and such. Our side's pretty much anybody who can hold down a steady job or two and keep the mortgage payments coming. Claytena's family's across the street on account of her daddy's a vice president at Chase or Citibank or Fleet or one of those banks. I can never get it straight no matter how many stickers and T-shirts and refrigerator magnets he comes home passing out. He works hard but is a bit partial to gambling. Between the gambling and his high-timey job, they stay right in the middle. Once in a while somebody'll start making noises about one side of the street thinking it's better than the other 'cause it's got more money or more grass or two cars parked out front instead of one, but for the most part people say good morning and how do you do to each other, get together and drink some nights, and pretty much just live.

We put the baby up in the guest room after she cries herself out. Ms. Williams is sitting at the kitchen table crying and me and Claytena go about fixing up some cheese and crackers and whatever else we can get our hands on quick enough to keep Mama from lighting into me.

"You work hard your whole life," Ms. Williams says.

"You sure do," Mama says.

"And the Lord's got other plans."

"He's got plans for all of us," Mama says. "From the cradle to the grave."

"From the cradle to the grave," Ms. Williams says.

It goes back and forth like that for some time, breaking up a bit every time Ms. Williams needs to blow her nose or let out a deep sigh. Her hands are shaking like they don't belong to her. Mama sets a small glass of rum in front of her and she sips it real fast. After a while, the shaking slows down. Ms. Williams lifts the empty glass up to her lips and gives the bottom of it a tap with her finger.

"I'd like another little taste of that," she says.

Mama frowns at me and I bring Daddy's bottle over and set it down beside her glass. She looks up at me, grateful like. She's a pretty woman, Ms. Williams is, gray-green-eyed like Chuck and curly headed. Mr. Williams and the baby are kind of square faced. He always makes me think of those men selling Marlboro cigarettes. I guess I get that idea because Chuck used to say that's what his daddy did—sold cigarettes for Marlboro—but anyone with half a brain knows none of those cowboy models are ever black. I asked Chuck when was the last time he looked up at one of those posters and saw a black man twirling a lasso. He looked at me like I was crazy. Later on, we found out his daddy sold advertising and such.

Me, Chuck, and Claytena seem to go back before we were born—when our mamas and daddies were looking for nice places to raise families and settled in on this street. This summer though, even though we've all been friends forever, everybody seems to be going their own way. Chuck's hanging with some raggedy old boys who live across town—and Claytena's all of a sudden all moony eyed over Chuck. Me, I'm thinking about ways to make it off this street—maybe go to another country. Someplace far away. I got an itch this summer, something deep inside me burning. Some nights I wake up all sweaty and just sit there waiting for whatever is coming on to just get to getting. Claytena says she feels the itch, too—when she's kissing on Chuck mostly.

"Figure Justin's too upset to sit down a moment and stop feeling bad about the fire," Ms. Williams is saying.

Mama frowns but doesn't say anything.

"He's real sensitive, my husband is. This'll hit him hard."

"They know how it got started?" Mama asks.

"They have some ideas. Say it blazed up too fast to be an accident. But I don't think kids would want to do something like that. Firemen say they can trace arson but they need to do a little more investigating. I don't believe someone would start a fire in our house and we just right down the street. More likely one of Justin's old nasty cigarettes."

The window is open and there's the tiniest bit of a breeze blowing in. When I lean my head out, I can see that teenager girl talking to Mr. Williams. I see he's got his head leaning into her like they've known each other for a long time. And I see she's got her own head kind of down and sideways, like she's telling him something about herself. I feel myself getting tiny and numb. When I was little, I used to always play with matches. I'd light two, three, four at one time and just hold them out in front of me and watch them burn. There was something amazing about the flame—the way it would dance and reach up all over the place. Once, I set the roll of toilet tissue on fire in the bathroom.

I didn't know it would catch as fast as it did and by the time my mama and dad got to the door, I was screaming, afraid I'd go up that quick—and just burn, burn, burn.

After a while I see Mr. Williams is making his way down the street, the teenager walking a few steps behind him.

"Girl, get your head inside that window and stop acting like you don't have any sense," my mama says. I duck my head inside and pull the window down.

Claytena puts the cheese and crackers in the middle of the table, laid out nice with some olives and the cheese knife kind of in the center of things. She sits down and I sit down across from her and we just all four sit silent for a while, nobody really looking at anybody else. In the back of my mind I can see Mr. Williams getting in the car with that teenager and driving off. I don't want to think about it but the thought keeps splashing around inside my head—all silver and blue and big as Mr. Wheeler's pool.

Outside, I can hear somebody yelling. Underneath it all, it's a pretty afternoon—one of those middle-of-summer days when the sun's buttering everything.

"You got your fire insurance covering it all," Mama's saying. "Time you get the first check, you'll probably be half finished renovating. Fireman said wasn't as bad as it looks. Get the smoke out of everything, you'll hardly know it was a fire."

"I'll know there was a fire all right, Eva. You can get the smoke out of the clothes, you can't get it out of your eyes." She kind of smiles at her own saying then pours a third taste of rum.

Claytena slides her eyes over to me then back to the rum bottle. I nod. By the end of the day, Ms. Williams will probably be passed out drunk—her mind far away from the fire and whatever else she's trying not to think about.

"Well, you know you welcome to stay here for as long as you need to," Mama says. "My girl could go stay with Claytena for a while, put Chuck and the baby in there, and you and Justin could take the guest room."

Ms. Williams kind of twirls her rum around with one finger. Her eyes are starting to smoke over. I can see her jaw muscle working itself back and forth underneath her skin but she doesn't say anything for a long time.

"Maybe you girls got somewhere else to be," Mama says and me and Claytena get up from the kitchen table and head back outside.

✳ ✳ ✳

"That teenager went off with Mr. Williams," I say when Clay and I are back on the fence.

The Williamses' house looks beautiful-ugly in the late afternoon. There are dark rings around the windows. The maple door is laying across the porch, sprinkled with glass. Piles and piles of clothes cover the grass. In the corner of the yard, I can see Chuck, holding something in his hand and just staring down at it.

Claytena sees him, too, and jumps down, then leans back against the fence and wraps her arm around one of the posts like she needs it to hold her up.

"I should go over there, huh?"

"I think she started the fire, Clay. That teenager."

"He's sitting all alone. I think he needs me."

Chuck is sitting in his driveway, his head down, a burnt-up-looking doll in his hands. Down the street Mr. Wheeler is taking the garbage out. He stops, still holding the trash bag, and looks over at Chuck, then turns and takes the garbage back inside. I can hear little girls singing "Miss Lucy had a baby she named him Tiny Tim . . ." And someplace farther away, a lady is laughing.

"You think I should go?" Claytena is asking.

I stare down at my fingers and nod. Then Claytena is running across the street and sitting down beside Chuck. She puts her arms around him and Chuck starts shaking. Crying and shaking in Claytena Smalls' arms.

When we were little, my daddy used to always take us to the amusement park in July. Every Saturday, we'd pile into his car and drive for a long time until we saw the Ferris wheel slowly turning. Me and Claytena and Chuck always got on the same rides and we'd stay on them until we were dizzy or nauseous or just plain tired of it all. Then we'd go to the next one and do the same thing—all day long until it was time to go home.

I climb off the fence and head away from them, walking slowly until I am off of our street, until the trees and houses and children become unfamiliar. The sun is almost gone now. I can hear crickets chirping and a crow. I can hear mamas calling their kids in for dinner and kids not wanting to leave their friends for the night.

And somewhere in the far back of my mind, I hear the amusement park hawker asking if anyone wants to take another ride.

Jacqueline Woodson on censorship

The thing about censorship is—one doesn't always know when it's happening. You walk into your library looking for a certain book and it isn't there. Is that censorship or the fact that the library couldn't afford to buy it this time around? You walk into your classroom and notice only certain kinds of books on the shelf. Is that censorship or a teacher's aesthetic? Censorship has played this sort of nebulous role in my life.

Then, there are times when it is obvious. Once I received a stack of letters from sixth-graders telling me why I shouldn't write a certain book they heard (from their teachers) was being published. Once an illustrator refused to illustrate the cover of a novel of mine because she found it "offensive." More scary than both of these examples is the silence—the not knowing what is being said and done about your work behind closed doors. In the case of censorship, the person under attack is usually the last to know.

From a very young age I knew that there were going to be people out there who didn't like me because of some sort of prejudice. I did not know the many ways in which their hatred could exist. I did not know it would enter into the most sacred part of me—my writing.

As a child and young adult, I wrote for myself, to get a better sense of the world around me, to be happy. I have gone back to that beginning, to the place from which my work began, and have once again found my solace in the writing. Like the censorship, like racism and homophobia and all the other hatreds in the world, the writing, too, will always be here—giving me a better sense of the world around me, helping me to grow and understand.

"I want to stay with you."

"I'm no place, man. I'm out there, you know. It's no place for a kid. You're going to a real family. You're going to like it."

He leaned against my shoulder. "A-ron, come with me."

"I can't do that, it's against the rules. Besides they just want you. Not me."

You Come, Too, A-Ron

by
Harry Mazer

I banged on the door to Placement. Locked. Outside, where I was, it was flat-out blowing snow. And cold. Last time I was here they'd tried hard to find me a family. And failed. They sent me up to Oakmont, a state school in the boonies. Too many kids, not enough staff. I had to watch my back every second. I skipped out soon as the peepers in the ditches started to sound in the spring. I never heard peepers before. Somebody had to tell me they were little frogs.

I banged on the door again, kicked it. I was shivering. I kicked the door really hard. Finally someone came and let me in.

I went straight for the radiator. *Ummmmmmm.* That heat! I could've stayed there all winter. The heat melted the snow off my jacket and it must have melted my brain because I started hoping that maybe, this time, they'd have somebody for me, a mother, who would call me to the table with the rest of her kids. I was flat-out, make-believe dreaming. I didn't admire myself for it. Gotta stay in touch with reality.

The woman at the reception window was watching me, never took her eyes off me. I don't like being watched. I like to think I'm like an animal at night that nobody sees. But everything leaves a mark. I found that out when I slept in the park. Even snakes flatten the grass where they slide.

I got so hot standing by the radiator I had to unzip my jacket. The woman in the window said, "Where you from? What's your name?"

"Aaron."

"Last name first."

"Hill."

"Address?"

I shrugged. I had no address. No house either.

"Father's name?"

I gave her my mother's name. A lot of good it would do. My mother was too messed up to stand for much. Never had the knack to keep a guy around. No make-nice in her, no softness, no forgiveness. No ability to look at things with half-closed eyes and see the bigger picture. Plus, being crazy as a coot—and a screamer. She could barely stand having me around. She went for me with a knife once. Threw it at me. Zinged it past my face. If I hadn't been on my toes, she would have sliced me up like a piece of bologna. They came and got her, sent her upstate. They put her on something that quieted her down. Now she don't even talk. I go up to see her and she hardly knows me.

"You been here before?" the woman asked.

It crossed my mind to lie, but it's not a good idea to lie to these people. They get you. Maybe I hesitated a little, because I always think to lie, but then I don't. I said, "Yes."

"Yes, you have, or yes, you haven't?"

"A-hah."

"What's that mean? Yes or no?" She finally found me in the computer, found my client number, and sent me inside to see Mr. Posner. Mr. Poz. Mr. Positive.

The corridor smelled. Food and crap smells. Noisy, yelling kids, same as before. A tall girl was standing in the corridor by herself. Watching the door like she was waiting to go.

"Hey, Aaron," she said.

"Hey, Natalie." I knew her from before. She was the same as me, never could stand being inside, neither.

"Full house," Natalie said. "They got no place to put us." Then she told me how she'd gone home and her stepfather called the cops on her. They brought her here in cuffs.

"They don't want me, I don't care. It's still my house. I got more right there than he does."

"Hear you!" I said.

I saw Big Cara, another girl from before. She and some girls I didn't know were crowded together on the couch. More kids there, too, I never saw before.

Big Cara motioned to me. "Hey, Aaron, you want to meet my friend Latesha?" Latesha's black hair fell flat and shiny around her face. "Say hello to Aaron, Latesha."

Latesha never looked in my direction.

Big Cara sat on me one time, playful by accident, but hard on purpose. Came down hard enough for me to still feel it. I don't favor playful girls.

Mr. Posner was down the hall, checking where they were putting the little kids to bed. He was talking to Janice, one of the aides. Poz, same as before: belly, rumpled shirt, clipboard.

"Hey, Poz," I said.

"Aaron," he said, like I'd never left.

He'd grown a mustache that didn't quite cover a scar above his lip where some pissed-off kid had clipped him in the mouth with a coffee cup. One of those accidents.

"What happened at Oakmont?" Poz said. "I thought we had you all set."

"Not a good place," I said. "Supervision was bad. Too many fights. I didn't like it."

Mr. Posner checked his watch. "You come see me tomorrow morning in my office. Ten o'clock."

Janice walked back with me to the activity room. She put her arm around me. "You hungry, hon? Maybe there's something left. Pizza there a while ago."

Big Cara and her friends were still on the couch, legs twined together like they were too cool to contemplate. Natalie was watching some kids playing a computer game. On the hospitality table there were some soda bottles and a bunch of cleaned-out pizza boxes.

"Too late," Big Cara called out.

I perched on the windowsill. Janice was rounding up more kids for bed, handing out pillows and chocolate bars. I got me a chocolate bar, too.

The girls on the couch were teasing one of the little kids. They wanted his cap. He was wearing red sweats. The top went down to his knees.

I peered out through the blinds. Dark out, the wind and snow blowing straight down the street. Better in here than out there.

"Hey, Kenny baby," a girl called. "C'mere, Kenny baby, let me see that cap."

The kid had it pulled down so low he didn't hardly show any face. A girl in wearing tight jeans came up behind him and snatched his cap off.

She put it on, tried it different ways, with her hair tucked in then out all around. "How do I look?"

"You're ugly, Patches," Latesha said. "Throw it here." She tried the cap on, then she handed it to Big Cara, who threw it to Patches.

The kid was running from one girl to the next, begging for his cap. "Give it," he said. "Give it." Back and forth. He was going nuts. The girls kept throwing the cap over his head. I don't know how the cap ended up in my hands. I didn't want it. It was a stupid game.

"Over here, Aaron," Latesha signaled to me.

"Give it." The kid was breathing like he was trying not to cry, blowing his thick, sugary kid breath in my face.

"You want it?" I said and gave him the cap. I saw his face for a second, his big, baby eyes full of tears, as he pulled it on.

"What did you do that for, idiot?" Patches threw a soda can at me.

I caught it, then tossed it back to her but softly. I was cool. Like, Come on, what are you getting so uptight about?

The kid hung with me after that. He wouldn't go, even when Janice called him out. "Aaron," the kid kept saying, only he pronounced it *A-ron*. "A-ron, is that your name?"

"A-ron," Patches said. "His name is A-ron like Mo-ron."

"Go," I said to the kid. Janice was waiting for him.

"You come, too, A-ron." He wouldn't go without me.

"Aaron's going to sleep with the babies." Patches laughed. They all laughed, even Natalie.

"Thanks for helping me out, Aaron," Janice said as we went down the hall. She lowered her voice. "Kenny and his mom were burned out of their house. His mom's in the hospital."

They had some cots for the boys down at the end of the corridor. Janice handed Kenny a pillow and a blanket. He wouldn't lie down till I lay down on the cot next to him. "You sleep there, A-ron," he said.

I closed my eyes. "I'm going to sleep," I said. "Now you go to sleep." More pizzas had been brought in. I could smell them. I wanted to get back before those girls ate them all.

The kid kicked the blanket off, then pulled it on again.

"Tell me a story," he said.

I told him a story about some rats that used to live in our house on Burke Avenue. "No Poppa Rat, just Momma Rat and six little rat babies. They were all over the place."

"Where did they sleep?" the kid asked. "With momma rat?"

"Right. In one big ratty bed."

"They got names?"

"Names A, B, C. The oldest was A, then came B, then came C."

"Then comes D, E, and F?"

"That's right, you know your letters. That way Momma Rat knew if anyone was missing. F was always slipping into the toilet and having to be fished out."

"How?"

"Soup strainer."

"Soup strainer?"

"That's how you pick up a wet rat."

The kid's eyes were closing. I started to go. He woke up. "Where's Burke Avenue?"

"Next to Bronx Park."

"We going to go there?"

"Sure."

"When?"

"Tomorrow."

"Promise?"

"Hey, no promises. It's a maybe." A big maybe, I said to myself. I put my hand on his head and held it there. "You go to sleep now."

＊　＊　＊

"Here's the baby-sitter," Big Cara yelled when I got back to the activity room. "You going to put me to bed next?"

I got a couple of slices of pizza and sat back on the windowsill. I could feel the cold on my butt. Last night, this time, I was in the bowling alley, sleeping in the coatroom till they turned on the light and found me. When I didn't leave, they called a cop.

Big cop, standing by the cigarette machine. Talking to me, asking me how I was doing and did I need a place to sleep. I kept my eyes fixed on the shiny bracelets on his belt. When he tried to grab me, I ducked past him and out a door.

"Hey, Aaron," Big Cara said. "How come you're so stuck up?"

I didn't answer.

"So you admit it."

"I don't admit nothing. If you're rich, you can be stuck up. Or famous. I ain't got nothing to be stuck up about."

They all thought that was funny.

"You got something that's stuck up," Patches said. Then they really screamed. Pushed out their chests. The whole line of them pushing out their boobs. "What about them stuck ups, Aaron?"

I could feel the heat rise to my ears, but I kept a stone face.

"How long you staying, Natalie?" Big Cara said.

"How long *you* staying?"

"Till they find me the right placement."

"There ain't no right placement," Natalie said. "We're too old and too miserable for people. And too ugly."

"My boyfriend thinks I'm cute," Big Cara said.

"With his eyes open or shut?" Patches said.

"He don't have to see me to know I'm cute."

They slapped hands.

* * *

The next morning when I woke up the kid was standing by my cot. He didn't shake me or nothing, but I could feel him there hanging over me. I cracked one eye open. "You going to eat, A-ron?" he said. He had that cap on.

I shut my eyes.

"I'm hungry, A-ron."

"Go eat, then." I shut my eyes, but all I could think of was them hungry girls. I had to get up and get my share. The kid came with me.

They had dry cereal and milk and doughnuts and coffee set out in the activity room. Kenny took everything I took, then sat by me, watching every bite I took. He ate what I ate, just the way I was eating it. It made me remember when I was little how I used to admire the big kids on Burke Avenue. I'd watch them in the playground, on the basketball court. We could never get on the court when the big kids were playing. Once, one of them gave me a comic. Just handed it to me. That was Dennis. He did things. He never talked to me or nothing. It wasn't like I was his friend or nothing. I'd see him on the corner, sometimes, hanging with his gang and he'd give me a wink.

Ten o'clock, I went over to Poz's office. Guess who was behind me? "You can't come in," I said. The kid just slid down against the wall in the corridor and waited.

In the office Poz was on the phone. A sign on the wall said

KIDS MATTER. I stood by the window looking out at a tree, a wet brick wall, a man brushing snow from the top of his car. Money to be made out there. I could help him get his car free. Maybe get a ride somewhere. There was freedom out there.

"Aaron." Poz was off the phone. "Sit down, here," he said pointing to the chair by his desk. "Let's talk about you."

I sat, stuck my feet out, jammed my hands in my pockets. Mr. Cool, that was me.

"Kenny likes you."

"He's nothing to me."

"He's going out today. Nice little kid. It's you big guys I'm having trouble finding a place for."

"Can I have a cigarette?" Poz had an open pack on the desk.

He handed me one. "Keep it out of sight," he said. "I can't be giving cigarettes to everyone. I don't have anything for you, Aaron, except Oakmont. What I want to know from you is, are you going to stay? What are your intentions?"

I tucked the cigarette in my shirt pocket. My intentions? That's what they always said. As if I had a choice.

"Right now, my intention is to go outside and have a smoke."

"I'd like to see you back in school, back on track, Aaron. Keep drifting, and before you know it, you'll be off the screen. You need your education. You have to stay focused if you want to stay in contention. It's not easy out there, you know that. I don't have to tell you. You've got a head on your shoulders. You should be using it." He smoothed his little mustache. "How's that sound to you, Aaron?"

"Okay."

"Then we'll go back to Oakmont?"

"I don't like that place."

"It's not perfect, I know, but they're willing to take you back. It's not that long. Just settle down, do your schoolwork, keep your eye on what's important. Just stay out of trouble."

Poz was doing his job. I didn't hold it against him. But he wasn't going to Oakmont with me. He didn't have to live there. "Thanks," I said, "but no. Give the spot to somebody else. I'm never going back there."

Mr. Posner threw up his hands. "Okay. Okay, Aaron. I don't know what I can do. I'll try."

* * *

I went outside to smoke. Patches was out there, too. She gave me a light. Then a guy wearing a tie came outside looking for me. "You Aaron? Janice wants you."

Inside, by the front door, I saw Janice with Kenny. He was sitting on the floor with the top of his sweats pulled over his head.

"He wants you," Janice said.

They all looked at me. Janice and the guy with the tie, and even the taxi driver who had come in and wanted to know what was holding things up. "Just talk to him," Janice said.

"Hey, Kenny." I nudged his sneaker. "What's happening, man?" I felt like a fool with everyone watching me. "Come on, Kenny." What was I supposed to do, carry him out to the car?

Kenny peeked out at me. "You said we were going to Bronx Park today, A-ron."

I knelt down in front of him, close, making a private place. "Remember what I said? It wasn't a promise, it was a maybe."

"I want to stay with you."

"I'm no place, man. I'm out there, you know. It's no place for a kid. You're going to a real family. You're going to like it."

He leaned against my shoulder. "A-ron, come with me."

"I can't do that, it's against the rules. Besides they just want you. Not me."

It made me mad as I said it. What was the matter with him? Kids here dying for a chance like this.

"Listen, butthead," I said, "you're going to live in a house with heat in it, with a bed of your own, a refrigerator you can eat out of any time you want, and a TV set in your room. How many chances do you think you're going to get?"

I was sounding like Poz, now.

The kid rubbed my arm. "You want me to go there, A-ron?"

"Hey, it's not for me. It don't matter to me, one way or the other."

"If I go there, will you come see me?"

"How'm I going to do that?"

"Drive."

"Where'm I going to get a car?"

"You can take a taxi."

"Sure. Just to see you."

"I'll give you some money."

"How much you got?"

He dug in his pocket and handed me a quarter with this big smile. Even he knew that was nothing.

"Wow, big coin." I flipped it in the air. "Tell you what I'll do. I'm going to get your phone number from Janice and call you up with this coin."

"And then we'll go to the park?"

"You never stop, do you? Yeah," I said, "I'm going to come see you."

"And we'll go see the rat family."

"Aaron is as good as his word," Janice said.

"Promise?"

I gave him a special handshake. "That's a promise handshake," I said.

* * *

I went outside with Kenny and he got in the cab. The guy with the tie got in with him. "Thanks, Aaron," he said.

I leaned in on the kid's side. "Talk to you soon, man," I said.

"Uh-huh." He had the cap pulled down again.

The taxi went down the street. Everyone went back in, but I stayed outside. The street was wide open. Nothing, nobody to stop me. Go! I said. My heart raced ahead, but my feet were dragging.

It was going to get dark soon. And cold. I'd have to figure out a place to stay. I fingered the quarter in my pocket. Find something to eat. Figure everything. So what were my intentions?

No intentions except maybe call Kenny. I'd have to find a phone. If I hadn't eaten up the quarter by then.

I remembered I still didn't have the kid's phone number. I had to go back inside and get that. And I remembered something else. There were phones at Oakmont. If I was there, the kid could call me whenever he wanted.

On weekends I could go see Kenny. Oakmont ran a bus into the city for kids visiting their families. I'd go see the kid. We'd go to Bronx Park, walk over to the zoo, and see all the relatives of the rats who used to live in my house. Me and the kid.

I went back inside. I didn't think about it that much. First, I'd find Janice and get Kenny's phone number. Then I'd go find Poz and tell him my latest intentions.

I struggle each day not to let the fear of the censor poison my writing. Where the censor rules, a dull sameness creeps into books. Am I becoming cautious, being too careful in what I choose to write about, watching my language? It's this caution inside that I fear, more than the censors. If I can't write the book that I want to write, what am I doing?

At a school board meeting in a town in Minnesota, my book *The Last Mission* was challenged because of its language. It's a war book, and its language is the language of war. I believe that if we want to read about the real world we also must accept the language of that world. Board members, rather than utter the offending words, wrote them on slips of paper, then passed them to each other under the table. The book was removed from the school shelves.

In Rochester, New York, two mothers of eighth-grade boys found forty-six objectionable words in a 182-page book. One of the words was "retard." The book, *The War on Villa Street,* was both fiercely attacked and defended in the newspapers and on television. The demand for the book was so great there wasn't a copy to be found in Rochester. But, as with *The Last Mission,* the book was kept out of the middle school.

In Des Moines, Iowa, the wife of a Church of God minister complained that the language and description of a sexual encounter between two teenagers in *I Love You, Stupid!* made the book morally inappropriate for high school students. The book was removed from the middle school but allowed in the high school.

Censorship is always negative, but there have been some

positive outcomes from the challenges to my books: The issues involved were now out in the open. The response to the censors was plain and clear: Back off. Read or not read what you want, but don't try to force your views on our kids.

The negative effects of censorship don't always come out in the open. Where have my books been quietly removed from school shelves without any voices raised in protest? Where has a librarian or teacher chosen not to order my books rather than risk arousing the censor? This closet censorship is difficult to gauge. Are we gaining against the censors? Are we losing ground? I don't know the answers.

Good books are created when authors can write freely, take risks, go where their imaginations lead them. Once the author begins to temper his language and writes not to his own standard, but to the standard of the feared censor, the quality of his work suffers.

Books belong to all who read. Readers need and want well-written, interesting books. And since what interests me may not interest you, we need more books. More authors. More varied points of view. Books are our windows on the world. They permit us to safely experience other lives and ways of thinking and feeling. Books give us a glimmer of the complexity and wonder of life. All this, the censor would deny us.

I know it's too hard. It's too hard to see her wasted on the bed. Everything that was to be known was crammed into the small space between us. We've walked together into the maze of our lives and have taken different routes. The beast has come to the reunion.

The Beast Is in the Labyrinth

by
Walter Dean Myers

My sister's name is Temmi. My name is John. When I was born my father gave me the name of Jon. Without the *h*. When I grew up and realized that he had never lived with us, had never been a father to us, I put the *h* back into my name. It's a small thing, something that many people would consider superficial, even dumb. But somehow I imagined him, *him* being my father, thinking it clever to leave out the *h*. Perhaps it reminded him of a friend he had known in the army, although I doubt that he was ever in the army. My mother doesn't speak of it when she speaks of him.

I applied only to out-of-town colleges. I wanted to get away from the streets I knew, from the people I knew, from the stench of garbage that came to me on the morning air. I received a scholarship from a small college in Millersville, Pennsylvania. There are cows in Millersville, and people with round white faces who eat too much and smile too much and expect too much of black seventeen-year-olds from Harlem.

Still, I like Millersville and I've made an investment here. I go to the pizza parlor on Saturday nights with the crowd from my dorm. I go to the diner across from the small airport and eat large German sausages and hard fried eggs. I've become part of the quota of blacks that Millersville finds acceptable. With the few of us on campus they can exercise their good intentions, their Christian feelings of warmth and brotherhood, without the doubt of challenge. In turn, I can accept their hospitality and their reaching out to me without wondering what it would be like if there were more of us.

Christmas break. I've come home and the sounds and sights and scents of Harlem meet me at the corner of 145th Street and Amsterdam. I walk down the hill toward my home and realize that my body is striving for a rhythm it hasn't felt for several months. Harlem. Home. Hard black faces. Hard black eyes watching like jackals for something ready to die. There's more. I see it, feel it, pull it from the streets into my heart. Harlem. Home. Children playing impossible games in the streets. The dirty city snow lining the curbs. Old men, warriors with only memories of their victories, shuffling through the concrete canyons of New York. Cave dwellers, Dogon villagers living in the shadow of the moon and remembering the labyrinth of their creation.

The labyrinth. Its echo first came to me in a field in Millersville. Me, blade thin, black, looking out over the sun-drenched field. Her, orange white, younger than she had the right to be, talking of dead European writers as if she were speaking a symphony. The labyrinth had started. Dozens of pathways that could lead to other places and other times came into my mind as if they had always been there. But they had not always been there and the knowing of it pulled at my shoulders.

* * *

Up the stairs I've run a thousand times. As a child running

from whatever bully had found me I had run up those stairs. As a ballplayer showing my strength I had run up those stairs. As a pretender looking for a better way I'd run up those stairs. Now I run up the stairs pretending I'm not apprehensive, that my testicles aren't drawn up in a hard knot anticipating the disappointment I know will come.

My mother opens the door. Brown skinned, prettier even than I'd remembered. There is a fragility about her, a sense that she's been wounded.

"Oh, it's so good to see you, son." The words come from her heart and suddenly I feel ashamed. Of course it's good to see me. I'm her son and she's my mother.

"I got a discount on the train," I say. Meaningless. What have I learned in college?

"You hungry?"

"Yes."

She offers food as a metaphor. I take it as poetry. We talk quietly. She doesn't mention my sister, Temmi. Neither do I. You don't go where you don't know.

"You meeting a lot of girls down there?" she asks.

"One or two," I say, grinning.

She turns her head slightly and gives me a look that says we must reestablish ourselves. My mind races to the next day. What will I do? Who will I talk to?

"How's Temmi?" The words slip out. I want to suck them back but they are loosed.

"She's sick," my mother says. She nods toward the bedroom door.

I stand and go to the door. The room is dark when I go in. I find the lamp and turn it on. Temmi is asleep. She is thin. On the night table there is a small plastic vial. I sit on the edge of the bed.

The labyrinth grows. There's a need to find a way out of despair.
I sense a distance between what I know and what I see before me.

"Yo, Sis."

She stirs. There's a white stain on her cheek. I rub her shoulder
and she moves under my hand. She turns in her sleep, and then
wakes with a jolt. She twists violently and starts to push herself
from the bed.

"John, when you get home?" she asks.

"Just now," I answer, smiling. I smile the reassuring smile I
have learned in Millersville. It doesn't change her suspicions.
"How've you been?"

"Okay." Her eyes dart around the room, looking for what I
might have seen.

She pulls open a drawer and takes out a stick of incense. The
smell of it will make me sick to my stomach. I mumble something about being tired and we both know everything there is to
know in our small world.

* * *

Daybreak somehow stumbles into the night, forcing its way
through the rooftops, and turning the darkness of the room to a
hard-edged gray. The shadow of the window gates forms a
medieval pattern on the wall. I look in the dresser and instantly
remember that I've taken all the decent underwear with me to
school.

In the bathroom. Voices from the kitchen. Soft, a conspiracy.
They don't want me to know what they are feeling. Me
in the mirror, toothbrush in hand. Me in the mirror, a
Prospero wannabe. In the kitchen. A pas de trois. Awkward

as we shift the weight around. I make instant resolutions.

"We ought to paint this place this summer. Do a whole number on it. Maybe paper the living room."

"I can design the paper," Temmi says.

"Nothing too far out," I say.

We talk and it's good. We drink tea and I wonder if there's coffee to be had. I don't ask because I really don't want to know. I want to walk away and think of better times. Times I will make better. Temmi says she has to go downtown to see about a job.

Luck is wished. We talk about the job and she leaves. Mom is relieved. I relax. The beast lurches.

*   *   *

Millersville. The teaching assistant is Irish. What he wants to talk about is Ireland at the turn of the century and how his grandfather used to stand across the street from University College and watch the gentlemen walk up the stairs into the school. What we want him to do is to amuse us with anecdotes about Joyce. About making the rounds of the pubs. About the white and flushing flesh of Molly Bloom. A round-faced, well-scrubbed literature major gets up the nerve to tell the TA what it is we want. He is hurt. He says we don't understand.

A phone call. Temmi hasn't been home for a week. The voice on the phone crackles with worry. All right, I'll come home.

*   *   *

"No, I ain't seen her," the corner monitor says. He looks up Malcolm X Boulevard, then checks the traffic on 135th Street. Nothing is amiss. His corner is safe. "I ain't seen you for a while, either. Where you been?"

"I'm going to school in Pennsylvania," I say.

"Hey, that's good," he says. But he looks at me carefully. Not long enough to dis me, just to see who I am. I used to be the guy who played ball with him. His mom used to shop with mine. He knew me then. He glances at me and says "Hey, that's good." But he looks at me carefully, just to see who I am.

I go downtown. Not the White downtown where we scavenged for jobs and other realities. I go downtown to 110th Street where old Harlem borders other sanities and where now a small buffer zone of young whites looking for cheap housing has been established. I find Pack in a barbershop.

I think: *What the hell are you doing out of jail?*

I say: "Yo, Pack, what's happening?"

"Hey, young blood, what's happening?"

"Same old thing," I say, reaching for an inflection that has become inflection instead of talk. "How you doing?"

"Lungs is working," Pack says. The scar on his cheek is lighter than his black skin, but somewhat heavier than original sin.

"Have you seen Temmi around?"

"Temmi? Your sister?"

"Yeah."

"She getting heavy, man." Pack looks across the street toward Central Park. "Getting heavy."

It's growing cold and a layer of fog covers the tops of the trees in the park. Our side of the park is beautiful, a respite from the probing angles of the city. The other side of the park, where it has a name, Central Park South, instead of a number, is a one-way entry into the labyrinth.

"Have you seen her around?" Are the words too softly spoken? Does he hear me? Can I force them out louder? "I lave you—"

"She hang out on 103rd sometimes," Pack says. "There's a bodega on the corner of 3rd Avenue."

I don't move. I nod but I don't move. No need to hurry. The corner will be there. The block will be there. I know the way. Ninety paces due East, then right turn past the burnt-out neon signs, back up past the building with the boarded windows, unless there are eyes peering from the cracks. If there are eyes then run quickly past until you reach the bicycle shop. Then west. Then south. Then, wherever. As long as you don't move too quickly you'll get there.

I get there.

"She went down the street."

Down the street. There is an open lot. Figures huddle around a garbage-can fire. Palms face the fire as if heat could radiate through thin brown arms. As if it's so cold a fire is needed. Beyond them, against the wall, a brown coat almost blends with the terra-cotta bricks. I walk over, my feet heavy on the gravel. Stop. Lean against the wall. She senses my presence and looks up.

There is a gesture. A kind of wave of the arm that stops halfway through its arc and collapses onto itself.

"How you doing?" I ask the lie.

She doesn't answer, which is the truth.

* * *

On the bus back to school the scenes flash before me out of order and I try to make sense of them. I want to make a list but the man sitting next to me would never understand so I try to put the scenes in order in my head. All the while the bus lurches through small New Jersey towns anchored by Elks' clubs and flag-draped firehouses.

There is a scene of me lifting Temmi to her feet. She stumbles against me. She stops and turns away. The sound of her retching does things with my stomach. There is a scene on the bus. The driver looks at me and at her. He smells the vomit and doesn't want it on his vehicle. He looks at me, imagines who I might be, and returns to his dreams of driving the bus.

There is a scene with my mother. She is making tea. She is putting a thin cover over Temmi's shoulders. She is making small, birdlike movements with her hands. Her lips move wordlessly. There are furrows between her eyes.

There is a scene with me in the doorway. I am lying words of reassurance. Necessary words.

But the scene that comes back again and again, never in order, is me and Temmi on the staircase. I am half walking her, half carrying her up the stairs. She stops and turns to me, her face incredibly luminous. She tenderly touches my cheek.

What does it mean?

The bus driver curses. I look up. There is a detour. The labyrinth grows denser.

* * *

"Yes." She looked at me and told me with her eyes to ask again and I did and she said "Yes."

Why the reaching for yes with this strange blond who thinks I am exotic? Why am I looking to bury myself away from wherever, whatever, it is I am from?

The days balance more precariously and I wake in the mornings full of the awareness that I do not want the burden of calling home. But I call, forcing the change into the coin slots, dialing the numbers, waiting for the familiar ring. Once. Twice. Three times.

"Hello?" Wary.

"Hello!" Cheerfully.

"Oh, hello." Small talk.

The pitch of her voice is high, and she speaks quickly. Things are good. She tells me about the new linoleum in the kitchen. It is light green and yellow. Real kitchen linoleum, she says, with squares of other colors. I think Mondrian.

I say that school is going well. She reminds me to study. How is Temmi? Better? I'm glad.

* * *

Spring break. The winter was too cold for my clothes. The spring has not come fast enough. After carefully making promises I will never keep I announce that I am on my way home.

"Where is home?" the TA throws the question above our heads, hoping it will somehow land on fertile ground. "Is it where the heart is, or from whence the soul has sprung? This is the question that Synge had to ask himself again and again."

"I was in Harlem once," someone named Jeff says. His father is an artist for a greeting card company. "I liked it."

No, you were never *in* Harlem, I think.

I get a ride with two girls who live in Meriden, Connecticut. Having long legs I sit in the front seat and we have good conversation all the way through Pennsylvania and into New Jersey. The girl in the back falls asleep as the rain starts and I imagine that the conversation is even better. I am running to safety without knowing what it is I am running from. The driver asks me if I have family. The answer is quick to come and warmly couched. It brings a glance and a smile to the driver's face and a description of her brother. He is smart and a good athlete. He collected coins but now has turned away from them. He is maturing, and that takes the smile away and brings a pensive look to a pretty face.

Why is Temmi so far away from this conversation? Why are her dark eyes like the memory of a memory?

We come through the Holland Tunnel and the car stops at Canal Street. The girl in the back is still asleep and so the kiss good-bye has more promise than it would have had. We are young and wondering about each other.

The D train shudders from the station, heading uptown. I have taken my laundry and placed it between my knees. There are resolutions to be fulfilled, walls to paint, a memo to myself to admire the linoleum. Yes, and in the laundry bag there is also a present, a set of four cups, saucers, sugar bowl, and creamer from an antique shop. They are of a translucent green glass. Carefully wrapped in Pennsylvania newspapers.

Mama opens the door and steps back to look at me. I stand taller and let her have her moment. I am glad to see her and reach out to her and pull her to me.

"Is everything all right?" she asks.

"Everything is wonderful," I say.

She looks at me again, giving me The Look that says I better be telling her the truth. Then she is satisfied that everything with me is wonderful and hugs me again. I think again how glad I am to see her.

Sitting on the side of the table nearest the stove she turns on the burner under the teapot. I take out the cups and saucers and unwrap them and she loves them. We talk at each other about the good things in our lives. Linoleum. Books. The diners in Millersville. How Mr. Givens down the street found God at last.

"How's Temmi?"

"Sick."

In the morning. That's when I'll go and see her. In the morning. Mom and I stay up most of the night, our voices becoming quieter as the night wears on. We hold the passing moments on our breaths and let them fall gently into the gathered darkness. There are smiles in our words as we remember each other fondly to ourselves. I see that the strands of gray in her hair have gathered themselves into streaks and hold their own character. I see that her hands are thinner. Fragile. We speak a language of family that is not quite real, but that we understand. I know for the first time that it is the understanding that matters, not the reality. We speak until my eyes are closed and I wake with a start, the green teacup still cradled in my hands.

It is morning. I walk to Harlem Hospital. There are corridors and guards. The corridor stinks of disinfectant. Doctors in green. Nurses in blue. Orderlies in white or green. Patients. Humanity shuffling through the halls.

A pass will allow me to go to the fourth floor, room 238. Mama said to tell her that she will come later. She has been coming twice a day. I think about telling her that Mama can't make it today.

Room 238 has five beds on one side of the room and five on the other. In the middle of the room a large cart carries what looks to be breakfast. The odor is unpleasant. Searching for Temmi I find her by the process of elimination. She is not the heavy woman with the heaving chest. She is not the bone-thin, white-haired woman staring off into space. She is not this one. She is not that one. I go to the far bed and find her lying on her side, facing the wall. There is an IV in her arm. Again she senses me. How does she do that? Is there some sense she has developed, some recognition of a kindred spirit? Of danger?

"Hello." I look into her eyes. I remember the Ancient Mariner, he of the glittering eyes. I don't want to look at what is left of her body.

Temmi struggles to sit up and I touch her shoulder. She moves her eyes away for a moment and then back to me. They plead. They plead and fill with tears.

"Oh, look at me," she says. Then her lips repeat the words but there is no sound.

She is ashamed. I don't want to sit on the bed and look around for a chair. The chair is white which I pull next to the bed. She takes my hand and holds it against her breasts. It makes me stay close to her which lets her look into my eyes. She reads me. Reads the truths my lips want to deny.

"Tell Mama not to come anymore," she says.

"You know I can't," I say.

"It's too hard."

I know it's too hard. It's too hard to see her wasted on the bed. Everything that was to be known was crammed into the small space between us. We've walked together into the maze of our lives and have taken different routes. The beast has come to the reunion.

I know it's too hard and she knows it's too hard for me. The words I search for don't come. The tower within me, the one that's been built with bricks of hope and the sure knowledge that there are things to do, collapses. I wonder if I'll be able to stand.

"Do you need anything?"

She shakes her head.

"I was thinking"—I hear the words coming from me and listen with interest—"that we could all move to Pennsylvania. Fresh starts and that kind of thing. Maybe we could change you into a Quaker."

She doesn't take her eyes from mine. Or my hand from her breast. I can feel her heartbeat, or think I can. After a long time I can't feel it, or think I can't.

So what is there to understand? That there are different places called home? That they're not easy to find, or to understand? That someone like Temmi might not have a home no matter how hard she looks?

I tell Mama I'll look for a place for her in Millersville. "It's a small town," I say. "There's not much to do and you'll probably have to learn to drive."

"At my age?" she laughs. Thin laugh lines touch the corners of her eyes. "What would I drive? A bicycle?"

*   *   *

Spring break is over. The funeral is over. The bus ride has ended. I swing off the bus and go into the waiting room in Millersville. Two guys are calling to another to hurry, the jitney to the college is about to leave. I run after them. They squeeze into the jitney and I decide to walk.

On the way to the dorm I think about waking up in Harlem the day after the funeral. Mom was up and washing the kitchen floor. It caught me by surprise and my first instinct was to pull the mop from her hand. Instead I went to the bathroom and washed. I caught a glimpse of myself in the mirror. Remembering how Temmi had looked at me I stepped closer and looked as hard as I could. There was nothing there that I could recognize, that I knew. Frightened, I turned away.

Later, we had tea in the green cups.

Still later, I said good-bye.

Walter Dean Myers on censorship

What are we to make of the idea that so many African-American writers confine their topic matter solely to issues concerning the black experience in the United States? We can believe that race is so exciting to these writers that they are compelled to explore it in every aspect and to limit their subjects to other African-Americans. Or we can believe that there is something very wrong with this picture. I believe that what is happening is censorship by omission.

This has been a quiet issue among African-American writers for decades. Langston Hughes, John A. Williams, and Zora Neale Hurston all spoke of the restraints placed on them as writers.

Limiting the ideas that will be published not only prevents the propagation of those ideas, it also corrupts the development of the writer. But censorship by omission does one other thing: It keeps the evils of censorship hidden not only from the general public but from other black writers who might be attracted to literature if they did not have to filter their thoughts solely through their racial identity.

The diner might have been brand new, but already it had a shabby run-down quality that made it fit right in with the neighborhood. It was two-thirds empty when we got there, and we had our choice of booths. Dad took one that faced the door, and sat in the seat where he could check who was coming in. He hadn't done that with me in a long time, and my stomach hurt in an old familiar way.

Ashes

by
Susan Beth Pfeffer

That winter, it felt like every time I saw my father, the sun cast off just a little more warmth than it had the day before. I don't remember a gray day when I saw him. Once it had snowed the night before, and getting to his apartment took longer than normal, as the buses inched their ways past snowbanks and awkwardly parked cars. But the sun made everything glisten, and the snow still had a pure look to it, which I knew would be gone by the following morning.

I saw him Tuesdays. I'd been seeing him Tuesdays for almost two years at that point. Before then, it had been Tuesdays and alternate weekends, but as my life got busier, weekends got harder, and Dad didn't complain when we fell instead into a Tuesday-evening ritual. Mom, who was still working on completing her degree, took Tuesday and Thursday evening classes, so I'd go straight to Dad's from school, wait for him to show, and then we'd have supper together and talk. It helped that he didn't live a hundred miles away. Just the other end of town, a two-bus-trip ride.

Dad drove me home Tuesday nights, and the moon always shone as brightly as the sun had and the winter stars looked joyful and beckoning. When I was little, Dad used to promise me the stars for a necklace, but like most of his promises, that one never quite happened.

"I'm a dreamer," he said to me more than once, which really wasn't all that different from what Mom said. "He's an irresponsible bum" was her way of wording it. I knew he was both, but I also knew that winter that the sun and the moon dreamed with him.

Sometimes when I haven't seen Dad for a few days, on a Saturday or a Sunday, I'll try to figure out why Mom ever married him. She's the most practical person I know, always putting aside for a rainy day. With Mom, there are a lot of rainy days and she takes a grim sort of pleasure in being ready for them. The flashlight with working batteries for a blackout. The extra quarters when the laundry isn't quite dry. The gift-wrapped bottle of wine for the unexpected and undesired Christmas guest. Her pocketbook overflows with tissues and tampons for anyone who might need them.

Dad gets by on a grin and a willingness to help. He's always there if you need him. Well, not always. He's unexpectedly there, like a warm day in January. He's a rescuer. "I saw a woman stranded on the road," he'd say. "So I changed her tire for her." Or he took the box of kittens to the Humane Society, or he found the wallet with the ID intact, and returned it in person to its owner (and, of course, turned down a reward). He helps blind people cross the street and lost people find their way.

"I go to bed at night, and ask myself, 'Is the world a better place because I exist?'" he told me once. "If I've done one thing, no matter how small, that made the world a better place, I'm satisfied."

Of course no one ever got rich helping blind people cross the street. The world might be a better place, but child support checks don't always show up on time, and I never did get that necklace made of stars. Both Mom and Dad see to it I know his limitations.

"All I can give you is dreams, Ashes," he said to me once. "But one good dream is worth a thousand flashlight batteries."

Ashes. I can still hear the fight. It was just a couple of months before the final breakup. I was in bed, allegedly asleep, when they went at it.

"Her name is Ashleigh!" Mom shouted. "A name you insisted on. So why do you call her 'Ashes'?"

"That's just my nickname for her," Dad replied. He was always harder to hear when they fought. The angrier Mom got, the lower his voice dropped. For some reason, that made her shout even louder.

"But ashes are cold, gray, dead things," Mom yelled. "You're calling your daughter something dead!"

"It's just a nickname," Dad repeated, a little quieter.

"You call her that just to annoy me!" Mom yelled, but Dad's reply was so soft, I could no longer hear him.

A couple of days later, when Dad forgot to pick me up at school, or didn't have the money for the class trip, or got all his favorite kinds of Chinese and none of Mom's and mine, I thought maybe Mom was right, and Dad did call me Ashes just to annoy her. I made a list that evening of all the words that rhymed with ashes—smashes and crashes, trashes and bashes, clashes and mashes—and it didn't seem quite so nice anymore, having a special nickname. But then Dad gave me roses or sang a song he'd written for me. Or maybe he moved two buses away. And I realized he still called me Ashes, where Mom couldn't hear him to be annoyed. And that made me feel special all over again. Mom might never be caught without batteries or tissues, but she just called me Ashleigh—a name she didn't even like—and never promised me anything.

"Mom, can I have an extra five dollars to go to the movies this weekend?"

"I can't promise you that."

What could Dad have promised her to get her to love him? And what could Mom have offered to make Dad love her back? Whatever it was, it was dying by the time I was born, and dead before I turned six. Dad could make everyone in the world smile, except Mom. And Mom was always prepared, except for what Dad did to her.

It was toward the end of February that winter, and the sun was shining and the air was crisp and clean. I sat waiting for Dad, who I knew would show up eventually. I probably did my homework, or maybe I looked out the window for his car to show. The room he was renting didn't have a TV. Maybe there was a library book to read. Maybe I folded his laundry.

When he got in, he was full of smiles and kisses and I no longer resented the waiting, if I had resented it at all. "Ashes!" he cried, as though it had been years since we'd last seen each other, and not a simple week of overcast skies and bone-chilling weather. "Have you ever seen such a day!"

I had, seven days before. But I smiled at Dad, who always seemed to discover the weather each time we visited.

"You look radiant," he said. "You get more and more beautiful. Turn around. Let me admire every single inch."

So I turned around. I was wearing jeans and a bulky brown sweater Mom had given me for Christmas.

"You could be a model," Dad said. "Have you thought about

that, Ashes. Modeling? Some of those supermodels make a fortune."

"Dad," I said. "I could never be a supermodel."

"Don't sell yourself short," he replied. "I've read interviews where they say they never thought they were pretty. Not in high school. Just tall and skinny. And you don't have to worry about being tall or skinny."

"I know, Dad," I said. "Which is why I'll never be a supermodel."

He looked at me and then he grinned. "All right," he said. "You're too smart for that kind of work anyway. Be a photographer instead, or a dress designer. You have flair, Ashes. Style. You do something like that, you're sure to make your mark."

Last week he'd told me to be an astronaut. The week before that, the CEO of a Fortune 500 corporation. And the week before that, he'd been stunned by my spirituality.

"Oh, Ashes," he said, taking off his winter coat and dropping it on the sofa bed. "I wish I deserved you."

"I wouldn't have any other dad," I told him. "My friends' fathers, they just tell my friends to study more. They never tell them they have flair or style."

"Maybe they don't," Dad said. "You're the special one, Ashes. You're the one-in-a-million girl."

"Am I really?" I asked, not needing the reassurance. I knew I wasn't a one-in-a-million girl, no matter how often Dad told me I was. But no matter how often he told me, I still loved hearing him say it.

"One in a million," he said. "And don't let anyone ever tell you otherwise, Ashes. They will, you know. They'll try to tear you down. They'll laugh at your dreams. Even your mother—and she's a saint to have put up with me all those years—even she will discourage you from being all you can be. I hate to speak against her, but she's not a dreamer, Ashes. She's the most level-headed woman I know. As straight as a yardstick. But I was the only dream she ever believed in and once I failed her, she never let herself dream again."

"Mom's all right," I said.

"She certainly is," Dad said. "She's a fine woman."

We were both silent as we pondered Mom. Then Dad laughed. "She'd never let you go hungry," he said. "What do you want for supper, Ashes? I can offer you pizza, Chinese, or fast."

"Anything," I said.

"No, no," he said, and he clapped his hands. "I remember. There's a new diner, opened right around the block. Let's treat ourselves, Ashes, and go out on the town."

"Can you afford it?" I asked, after doing the mental arithmetic of diner versus pizza.

"For a special date with my daughter?" he replied. "Of course I can afford it. Besides, I have something to celebrate."

"What?" I asked.

"I have a chance at something really big," he said. "All I need to do is put together a little financing, and I'll be set for life."

"For life?" I said, and I must have sounded like Mom because he stopped smiling.

"All right, not for life," he said. "But it'll be the start of something really big, Ashes. I can feel it. Just a couple hundred bucks, and then all the pieces will fall into place."

I had no idea where Dad thought he could get two hundred dollars. But he looked so happy I had to smile, too.

"Then diner it is," I said, and I got my coat. Dad picked his up from the sofa and put it back on. "Rice pudding for dessert," he said as we walked out the door. "You can always tell the quality of a diner by its rice pudding."

The diner might have been brand new, but already it had a shabby run-down quality that made it fit right in with the neighborhood. It was two-thirds empty when we got there, and we had our choice of booths. Dad took one that faced the door, and sat in the seat where he could check who was coming in. He hadn't done that with me in a long time, and my stomach hurt in an old familiar way.

"Waiting for someone?" I asked him. I stared at the menu, so I wouldn't have to look at him not looking at me.

"Of course not," he said. "Not when I'm with you. Take your pick, Ashes. Hamburger, triple-decker, chicken salad platter. Whatever you want."

I ordered the burger and fries, hoping that by the time it came I'd feel like eating. Dad took a quick look at the menu, closed it, and ordered coffee.

"You'll share my fries," I said to him.

He nodded as though we'd just completed a difficult negotiation. "I'll even eat your pickle," he said. But then he looked back at the door.

"What is it?" I asked him.

"It's nothing," he said. "Oh hell, Ashes, you can always see right through me."

He was the one who'd been looking right through me toward the door, but I didn't say anything.

"That money," he said. "The two hundred dollars?"

I nodded.

"Well it isn't so much for a deal as to help pay off one I

already made," Dad said. "But I've got to tell you, honey, once that money is paid, I'm on my way to easy street. Just a little setback. But you know how those guys are. They get itchy when you owe them money. And it's not always comfortable to be where they can scratch you."

"You owe them two hundred dollars?" I asked, trying to keep the panic out of my voice.

"Give or take," Dad said. "But don't worry about it, honey. I'll work it out. I always do."

My burger and fries came then. Dad took a long sip of his coffee, while I poured ketchup on my plate and twirled a fry in it. "Can I help?" I asked.

Dad smiled like I'd offered him the key to the mint. "I love you so much," he said. "You're ten thousand times better than I deserve, Ashes."

"Have a fry," I said, pushing my plate toward him. Dad took one. He seemed to have more of an appetite than I did.

"I had a thought," he said as he reached for my pickle. "Your mother keeps a couple hundred in cash at her place."

I didn't think either of us was supposed to know that.

"In that pretty teapot her mother gave her," Dad said. "Unless she's changed her hiding place. I know she changed the locks when I moved out, so maybe she changed her hiding place as well."

Sometimes, when Mom wasn't home, I'd take the lid off the teapot and stare into it, imagining what I could do with two hundred dollars. I looked at Dad and realized he'd had those same fantasies. Well, why not. I was his daughter, after all.

"The money's still in the teapot," I said.

Dad grinned. "She's a wonderful woman," he said. "But she gets one idea and she never wants to change it."

"What do you want to do, Dad?" I asked. "Come into the apartment with me and take the money?"

"Oh no," he said, and he looked really shocked. "That would be robbery, Ashes. I would never steal from your mother. I've caused her pain enough."

I took a bite of burger. Dad ate some more fries.

"No, I just thought maybe you could borrow the money," he said. "Just for a day or two, until I straighten out all my finances. Your mother would never know the difference. Unless there's an earthquake or the Martians invade. I think we can gamble neither of those things will happen before Friday."

"You'll be able to pay her back by Friday?" I asked

"You," Dad said. "I'd be borrowing the money from you. And I swear to you, Ashes, I'd have the money in your hands by Friday at the latest." He wiped his hand on his napkin and offered it to me as though to shake on the deal.

"Dad, I don't know," I said. "That's a lot of money. What if Mom finds out?"

"It's me she'd be angry at," Dad said. "Which is why she'll never find out. I wouldn't jeopardize our time together, honey. You let me have the money tonight, I'll straighten out my little difficulty, and Thursday night, when your mom is out, I'll give you back what I owe you. No earthquakes, no Martians, no problem."

I looked at the clock on the wall behind Dad. "Mom'll be home soon," I said.

"You all through?" he asked.

I nodded.

"Let's go, then," he said, the rice-pudding test long forgotten. We went back to his place so I could pick up my books. Then

we walked down to his car. "Why don't you sell your car?" I
asked him. If he did that, I'd keep my hands clean, and Mom
would never know. "You could get the money you need that
way."

"You're your mother's daughter," he said. "Good head on your
shoulders. Problem is, I'd never be able to find another car this
cheap to replace it. No, Ashes, the teapot's the way to go."

We drove back to Mom's in silence. Usually we talked.
Sometimes Dad sang one of his songs to me. For a moment, a
cloud drifted past the moon and the sky turned greenish gray.

"Snow tomorrow," Dad said. "Maybe you'll get a snow day."

"Maybe," I said.

Dad parked the car a block away from Mom's. "Just in case she
gets home early," he said. "I don't want her to see me waiting."

"Okay," I said.

"You go up to the apartment," he said. "Take the money, and
come right down. Then I'll drop you off in front of her place, like
always, and she'll never know the difference."

"What do I do if Mom's already there?" I asked.

"Just stay where you are," he said. "If you're not back here in
ten minutes, I'll go home."

"All right," I said, and reached to unlock the door.

Dad touched me on my shoulder, gloved hand on winter coat.
"You're one in a million," he said to me. "The best daughter a man
could dream of."

I got out of the car and ran over to the apartment. I took the
elevator to the tenth floor and unlocked the door. The apartment
was quiet. It always felt a little colder when Mom wasn't there.
Even with the lights turned on, it seemed a little darker.

I walked into the kitchen and turned on the light. The teapot was right where it belonged. I lifted its lid and stared at her emergency money. It was shaped like a little house, with a curtained window and a flowerpot on the windowsill. It was the sort of house I'd never lived in, probably never would with the amount of time it was taking Mom to finish her degree.

I stood over the teapot and stared at the money. Mom's emergency money. Her earthquake money. Her Martian money. Ten Andrew Jacksons stared right back at me. They offered me no advice on what I should do.

I looked out the window and saw only ash gray sky. In the cold stillness of the night, I could hear my father's car keening in the distance. "You're one in a million," it cried.

Susan Beth Pfeffer on censorship

When I was a senior in high school, I was the assistant literary editor of my school paper. I loved the job, which I mostly remember as counting numbers of letters to see if things would fit into column inches.

One day one of our writers suggested an editorial saying if you had study hall last period, you should be allowed to leave the school grounds. The teacher advisor sent the writer to the school principal, who vehemently (and apparently obnoxiously) forbade the paper to run such an editorial.

Years passed. I became a writer of novels for young adults. I decided to combine the censored editorial incident with an incident a friend had told me of working on an underground newspaper at her high school. I used my high school principal as the basis for the principal in the novel (*A Matter of Principle*), and used my eleventh-grade history teacher as the basis for the character of the teacher advisor (even though in real life, she'd had nothing to do with the paper; I just didn't like her so in she went).

It's easy enough to censor an article, a newspaper, even an idea. But no matter how hard you try, you cannot censor a mind or an imagination. You can never censor the future.

"I'm gonna ask you the most important question there is in the whole world," Paul Creese finally said. "You're not a boy anymore, but are you a man?"

Baseball Camp

by
David Klass

We sat on the mud and grass between the third-base line and the dugout and watched him in silence. There were twenty of us—all teenagers, the oldest group at the camp. From the second diamond, a hundred yards away, came the shouts of the mid-level campers, already divided up and playing a scrimmage. Beyond them, nearest to the one-story green camp bunkhouses, the Little Leaguers practiced shagging outfield flies on their own small baseball diamond.

"Any of you ever hear 'bout Tyrus Raymond Cobb?" the big man demanded. "Not such a bad man. Gave money to build a hospital. Did a lotta nice things. But that was after he retired. When he played the game he used to sharpen his spikes. Know what that means?"

A few heads nodded, but most of us just sat there and tried to avoid the big man's eye. There was something menacing about him. He was nearly six-three, with a huge pot belly and a southern accent that colored every word out of his mouth. He had a game right leg so that he limped badly when he walked, and when he stood still his shoulders sloped slightly to one side. The large chaw of chewing tobacco in his mouth caused him to spit regularly, and he timed those occasions to nearly punctuate his story.

"Ty Cobb was the greatest ballplayer to ever play the game," he told us. "The greatest and the fiercest. You read 'bout him if you like to read. The Georgia Peach. Father was a preacher. One time one of Cobb's teammates on the Tigers went into the shower room ahead of him, and Cobb nearly killed him. 'I'm the best player on this team by a hundred miles' was all he'd say after they broke it up. 'I'm the best and it's right that I should shower first.' "

He broke off to run his eyes over us, and apparently he didn't like what he saw. He scowled as he muttered, "Damn, but you are the ugliest bunch of pencil necks ever assembled on a sand-lot."

I glanced down from him at the guys around me, and tried to find the ugliness that he was talking about. I saw a bunch of average-looking thirteen- to sixteen-year-olds in sweatpants and T-shirts. So far I knew only a few of them; there was Simon from Montreal and Roger from New York and the guy who slept on the bunk beneath me, Eric, from Cincinnati.

"Damn," he repeated again. He pointed to Eric, who looked nervously back at him. "What's your name, boy?"

"Eric."

"Call me 'sir.' Where're you from?"

"Cincinnati, sir."

"Don't they have barbers in Cincinnati?"

Eric looked back at him, unblinking.

"Wear your hair like a girl and no man's gonna take you seriously, son. How you gonna hit a baseball when you feel that way 'bout yourself?"

Eric lowered his eyes and his shoulder-length brown hair moved across his neck in the light breeze.

"My name's Creese," the big man said. "Paul Creese. I'm in charge of you for the next two weeks and I'm gonna see that you work your butts off. You'll learn the technical side of the game— the cutouts, the backups, the correct way to field your positions. I'll ride you hard 'cause that's the only way you're gonna get better. Most of you'll hate me by Wednesday, which don't bother me at all."

He moved his head around on his thick neck so that his sharp little black eyes seemed to challenge each of us personally. "You'll say Paul Creese is the biggest, fattest, meanest, most arrogant southern son of a bitch ever crossed your path. But I wanna leave you with one thought. You gotta be strong for football. You gotta be tall for basketball. You gotta speak a foreign language to be any good at soccer. But for baseball you just gotta believe in yourself. There're guys playin' in the Majors who're runts, but they have it here," and he tapped his forehead, "and here," and he tapped his heart. "Now everybody up and let's see you run six laps around this whole field. C'MON, GIT GOIN'!"

So we ran for him, and later we did push-ups and sit-ups for him, and when he let us we played a little baseball in front of him, always afraid that we would somehow make a mistake that would anger him to violence. He threw a bat at one guy who he thought was dogging it, and when Roger from New York didn't go all the way up on a sit-up Paul Creese made us run ten laps for punishment. By Wednesday we all hated him, and by Friday there were whispers of mutiny, but they were just whispers. No one dared to even talk back to him, let alone try to stand up to him.

On Sunday we played a nine-inning scrimmage against a local team, and we lost badly. Roger, our starting pitcher, had an attack of wildness in the second inning, and walked in two runs before Creese replaced him. After the game Creese had us gather in our usual spot on the grass. He had two boys with him—they looked to be about nine and ten. "These are my sons," he told us, an arm around each of them. "Tyrus Raymond and George Herman. You won't find a better pair of boys." The boys had crew cuts and perfect posture, and listened to their father speak without looking at him or at us. Both seemed to gaze out across the baseball field at the same invisible spot on the distant horizon.

"Too bad my boys had to witness that disgusting display," Creese told us. "Losing stinks. I hate the stench. Smells like a dead animal. Stand up, pencil neck." He pointed at Roger, who slowly stood. Roger was thick boned and slope shouldered, with greasy black hair and bad acne. He was from New York, and the rumor in camp was that he was from a very rich Long Island family. "Come closer," Creese said.

Roger walked over to him. The big man looked down and slowly scowled. "You walked in two runs today. Still think you're a pitcher?"

"Yes, sir," Roger answered. "I had a bad day."

The answer seemed to anger Paul Creese. The scowl on his face twisted till it almost looked like he was in pain. "Boy," he said, "you sure are ugly."

Roger didn't say anything.

"Ain't he ugly?" he asked George Herman.

"Yes, sir," George Herman answered.

"Walked in two runs, and a face like that in the bargain. I'm glad I'm not that ugly," Creese muttered.

"I don't think it's any of your business how I look, sir," Roger said back to him, loud enough for us all to hear.

There was a long silence, and the afternoon breeze scooped up the dust from the infield and swirled it into the air. Paul Creese's scowl slowly flattened out into a thin smile. "Well," he said. "Well. Ain't that just terrific."

Roger stood his ground. "I may have had a bad day on the mound but you don't have any right to insult me."

Paul Creese reached down suddenly and grabbed Roger's shirt and twisted it so that Roger had to stand on his tiptoes. The big man glared right into his face. "You talk back to me one more time and I'll whup you right here on the infield. Understand?"

I could tell how scared Roger was by the way his voice trembled as he said, "Okay, I understand. Please, let me go."

Paul Creese shoved him backward and he stumbled and fell. "Walked in two runs," he growled at the rest of us. "He's got good stuff, spots the ball pretty good, but when they loaded the bases did you see him come apart out there? Did you see how scared he was? Like a little girl walking through the woods by herself at night. If you don't have it in your heart, get the hell off the field."

He paused for breath, and when he spoke again his tone was different. "You all probably heard the story about when Babe Ruth called his home run. Pointed to the fence and then hit the next pitch right over the spot where he pointed. Greatest moment in American sports. Imagine, callin' a homer like that in the Major Leagues. But what you may not know is that after the game the reporters asked him what would'a happened if he'd missed? They pointed out to him how stupid he would'a looked if he'd swung and missed, or popped the ball up. You know what the Babe answered? Said he'd never thought of that—never con-

sidered it!" Paul Creese let a moment pass as if in silent rever-
ence. "Not 'cause he was stupid—'cause he believed in himself
so much that that was not even a possibility in his mind. Total
confidence. Do you see what I'm saying?"

We nodded. He glared down at Roger. "Pock face, do you see
what I'm trying to get across?"

"No, sir," Roger said. He seemed to have regained his com-
posure since being released. When he spoke, his voice rang with
a daring confidence. Watching him stare right back at Paul
Creese, I admired his guts as he said, "I think Babe Ruth probably didn't think about missing the ball because he wasn't very
bright. And my name's Roger."

"Don't push me, boy. I'm warning you."

"And I'm warning you. You have no right to touch any of us."

Paul Creese looked down at his sons. "You two boys go stand
over by home plate," he said. Then, to us, "Somebody put on a
mitt and get behind the plate. The rest of you come out to the
mound. I'm gonna show you something."

We followed him out to the mound. The sun was just starting
to sink in the west, dipping below a row of tall pines. He stood
on the mound and held a baseball loosely in his right hand. He
looked in at his sons, and shouted, "George Herman and Tyrus
Raymond, stand on either side of the plate, 'bout eight inches
apart. No, closer. Closer. That's it." The catcher's mitt just filled the
space between them.

"If either of you two move I'm gonna skin you alive," he
shouted to them. "Close your eyes if you have to. I want you like
rocks." Then he looked at us. "In my day, I threw in the low
nineties. Now, with this bum leg, maybe eighty."

He went into a set position, and the ball in his pitching

hand nearly disappeared into his fat stomach. Then, taking a short step because of his bad leg, he plunged forward and released the ball as a white blur. It streaked plateward, split the eight-inch gap between his two sons, and smacked loudly into the catcher's mitt. His younger son flinched slightly at the sound of the baseball hitting the mitt, but his older son didn't move a muscle.

Paul Creese turned to us. "Know why I can do that?" he asked. He tapped his heart. "I believe in myself. I know EXACTLY where I'm gonna throw the ball—couldn't possibly end up anywhere else. C'mere, Mr. Bigshot pitcher from New York."

Roger stepped a half step closer to the mound. They eyed one another in silence for several seconds. "I'm gonna ask you the most important question there is in the whole world," Paul Creese finally said. "You're not a boy anymore, but are you a man?" His voice dropped lower, but we could all still hear him. "Think you are? Do you have what it takes?"

"I think I have what it takes," Roger said.

Paul Creese flipped him the baseball. "Let's see it," he said. "If you throw one fastball between 'em I'll take my hat off to you. But if you hit one of my sons I'll have your hide. Let's see you do it. I did it—now you do it."

Roger held the baseball straight down toward the ground, as if it was a heavy weight. Looking right at Paul Creese, he stepped onto the mound and his feet found the edge of the rubber. He looked in at the target, then at Creese, then at the target again.

"Come on, boy," Paul Creese said, "don't acknowledge the possibility of failure. Let it go. Let it go. It's all a matter of confidence."

Roger seemed frozen on the mound in the twilight. His arms were locked at his sides, his elbows at his hips. Behind the plate, Paul Creese's two sons both had their eyes closed.

"No," Roger finally said, very faintly.

"THROW IT!" Creese commanded him.

Roger stepped off the mound and dropped the baseball. It rolled a few feet on the hard dirt and came to a stop. "No," he said looking right at Creese. "I've had enough of this." He took a step away, and then said, "Don't you touch me," as Paul Creese came after him. Roger turned to run, but he got his feet tangled up with each other and stumbled. Creese, moving with surprising speed, kicked him in the rear end with enough force to send him sprawling in the dirt. Roger got up and without a backward glance sprinted off the field in the direction of the bunkhouses.

Creese walked back to us and acted as if nothing had happened. "Don't need sunlight to run laps," he said. "C'mon. Ten laps before dinner." For a long moment we all sat there looking back at him. His voice sounded like it was coming through a megaphone as he barked, "I said LET'S GO. NOW, OR IT'LL BE TWENTY." Simon was the first off the bench, and then Eric joined him, and cowards that we were we soon were all running laps, strung out all along the perimeter of the field while Paul Creese glared at us through the twilight.

Roger didn't come to practice for the next two days. He came to meals and ate alone, and spent the rest of his time in our bunkhouse, reading the long novels he had brought with him in his duffel bag. We had another scrimmage coming up on Wednesday, and Paul Creese was working us so hard that we had little time to wonder what Roger was doing or to think about anything else but baseball.

On Tuesday night, after dinner, word came that Paul Creese

wanted to talk to us out by the ball field. It was chilly for summer, so I pulled on a sweatjacket over my T-shirt before jogging
out with everyone else to see what was up.

Paul Creese had been drinking. He must've had something
awfully strong during dinner, because he had been dead sober for
afternoon practice and now his movements were jerky and he
ran his words together.

We assembled at the bleachers, sitting on the lower two rows
as Paul Creese preferred. His two sons stood off to one side,
watching their father with blank but attentive faces. He stood in
front of us for a time, his shoulders swaying just a bit as he
inspected us one by one. "Boys," he finally said, "I have some sad
news. We have a squealer in the camp."

We all looked at each other, as if everyone was secretly afraid
that they would suddenly be accused of the heinous crime. Then,
gradually, all eyes turned back to Paul Creese.

"Know what a squealer is?" he asked us. "A pig. Know what
a pig is? Someone who only thinks for himself. Someone who's
that selfish. What do you know to act that way? What do any of
you know?" He tottered and almost went down.

"Paw?" his older son, Tyrus Raymond, said quietly from the
shadows. The sound of his son's voice seemed to revive Creese a
bit. He pulled a handkerchief out of his back pocket and wiped
his face, and then squeezed it into a ball in his right hand.

"It's a short story and a sad one, but you might as well hear
it," he said. "Boy from Valdosta, Georgia, was the best high school
pitcher in the United States of America. Threw in the low
nineties. Born to pitch, the newspaper said. Had a curve could
go around a corner, then turn around and come right back. Had
'Major League' stamped on his forehead." He was gripping the

wadded-up handkerchief like a baseball now—swinging his arm slightly back and forth as he talked. "Scouts used to come back to his house after the game and tell him and his parents 'bout the gold at the end of the rainbow. When the draft came, he went first, numero uno, to the New York Yankees."

He looked around at us, his face suddenly glowing like the big light strung up behind the backstop. "First round by the Yankees. Team of DiMaggio, team of Gehrig, team of Babe Ruth. And a week before spring training starts that eighteen-year-old boy is mowing his daddy's lawn and dreaming 'bout the games in big-city stadiums and the plane rides and he's hearing the crowd's applause in his ears, and suddenly his foot and ankle are sucked up into that mower and turned into hamburger."

He dropped the handkerchief and swallowed, and when he finally managed to speak again, his voice was angry. "Turns out that boy Roger's daddy is a big-shot lawyer in New York. Roger called his daddy, his daddy called the old lady who runs this camp, and I guess this is the last time I'll be speaking to you. I just wanted to tell you you were coming along. Not one of you's got a lick of talent and you're each uglier than a rat-eared mongrel dog, but you were gettin' a little better. It's all up here," he tapped his head, "and here," and he tapped his heart.

Then suddenly, with no warning, he exploded loudly. "DAMN THAT MAMA'S-BOY POCKED-FACE SLOB TO HELL. What does he know about anything, the ugly squealer? Sad thing is, he had the most talent of any of you by a hundred miles. I could'a taught that boy something. Not fair, that he should have the most talent. Not fair . . ." The big man's voice broke, and he turned away from us as he mumbled, "Why'd he have to go and make that phone call? He could'a been a ballplayer. He could'a been a pitcher."

Paul Creese swayed like he would go down, and started slowly off the field. His two sons hurried to him, and he put one arm around each of their shoulders for support, and made his way toward the camp buildings. None of us stirred or said a word. We just watched in silence as he limped away into the dark of the night.

on censorship

The two novels of mine that have generated the most controversy and attempts at censorship are the two novels I am most proud of: *Wrestling with Honor* and *California Blue.*

Wrestling with Honor contains a chapter where my main character, Ron, goes on a date with an aggressive girl who initiates a make-out session. Ron eventually calls a halt to it. When the novel was published, I received a number of outraged letters from school officials wanting to know why I had "ruined" a good novel by sticking in a "gratuitous sex scene." Several told me that because of that one chapter, they would not be ordering *Wrestling with Honor* for their school libraries.

This struck me as odd on three levels. First, I think *Wrestling with Honor* is the most moral book I have written. Ron grapples with questions of honor that go back two generations.

Second, the so-called "sex scene" is hardly X rated—it reflects a normal dating experience for a shy seventeen-year-old boy. I wrote back to one offended teacher: "Weren't you thinking about these things when you were in school? How can we expect teenagers to read novels if we avoid real-life situations?"

Finally, the chapter was in no way gratuitous. It helped to illustrate what a straight arrow Ron was, and how he adhered to his own strict and personal moral code, even in the face of temptation and pressure. I did not write it to sell copies of the book, but rather to help define my main character.

John Rodgers, the main character in *California Blue,* has a crush on his biology teacher. When the novel was published, I was attacked for treading on the taboo ground of a teacher-student flirtation, and told that the 'crush' subplot kept the novel from winning several prizes. To me, as a writer, the "crush" was a defining element of John's character. He would not have been the same awkward, brave, isolated young man without it.

When I write novels, the characters seem to exist on their own—they have their own integrity, their own strengths, their own flaws. I try to catch their voices, follow them through the story, and remain true to them. There is no way I can truthfully render characters if I must constantly worry about offending censors.

I feel very strongly that students do not need to be protected from books. People should learn to choose books for themselves, based on their own tastes and values.

The centipede froze on the ceiling, allowing Tuesday to relax and continue to secretly caress the crumpled size-ten-to-twelve ankle support she clutched in her hands. She slid her left hand into its elastic and stretched it, then slipped it over onto her right hand. Just touching its thick, pliant ribbing eased her back into the stupor of romance and prayer and coincidence that had recently absorbed her life. Too many extraordinary things had happened to her the last week for her not to believe there was some sort of blessed design and sweet sorcery to the universe.

Love and Centipedes

by
Paul Zindel

Tuesday Racinski's large green eyes glinted with concern as a three-inch furry centipede descended over the faded wallpaper storks of Madame Wu's. Her mother sat opposite her in the booth plunging serving spoons into pots of shark fin soup and shrimp with lobster sauce that lay between them like tiny steaming lakes. The girl waited until the long bug was nearly at eye level before she first broadcast her thoughts to it. *Hello, wee centipedie. Can you see me, little buggie? Can you hear what I'm thinking? Can you?*

The centipede stopped and pointed its antennae at her.

Don't come to our table, Tuesday's silent prayer continued. *Please don't. Please, sweet living thing, make a left turn and travel away from me. Climb back up the wall and go to Maureen Willoughby's booth.* Tuesday began giggling at the wickedness of her thoughts. *Go to Maureen, the great cheerleader from Tottenville High. Go to our most beautiful leader of cheers, and all her enchanting and perfect cheerleader friends. Go above their booth and drop onto their long sleek blond Country Club hairdos . . .*

The mother was focused on sucking the meat off a gingered beef rib as the daughter watched the bug's antennae swish gracefully through the air. It looked like the same sort of centipede that Tuesday had begun to see around her house, ones that seemed to come out of the bathroom and cellar drains.

For a moment the centipede stared back. It appeared to be listening to Tuesday's thoughts. Then it turned suddenly and rippled back up the wall. Its path was hyperbolic at first, followed by a series of sharp, dizzying zigzags when it scooted across the ceiling. Eventually, it stopped its journey just above Maureen Willoughby's booth.

No, Tuesday broadcast. *No, bug. Stop. I've changed my mind. Don't drop. Maureen will only scream and Madame Wu's will get in trouble with the Board of Health, and the bleached cheerleaders will all jump up and down and try to stick you with a fork.*

The centipede froze on the ceiling, allowing Tuesday to relax and continue to secretly caress the crumpled size-ten-to-twelve ankle support she clutched in her hands. She slid her left hand into its elastic and stretched it, then slipped it over onto her right hand. Just touching its thick, pliant ribbing eased her back into the stupor of romance and prayer and coincidence that had recently absorbed her life. Too many extraordinary things had happened to her the last week for her not to believe there was some sort of blessed design and sweet sorcery to the universe.

It had all begun when she was assigned Maureen Willoughby's boyfriend as a science-project partner. Kyle Ecneps: handsome, his skin clear and beautiful; his eyes and his lips glow. He was a prince who'd come each day to Tuesday's cellar to work at her side on their experiment. Kyle Ecneps was the proof that there were things such as miracles and angels and riddles.

A daydream of Kyle grabbed hold of Tuesday's mind there in the booth at Madame Wu's. It happened like a hallowed replay, a type of true-life MTV video spinning in her head.

"My feet hurt from track," Kyle had said in Tuesday's cellar. "The coach made us run three miles today. I had cramps from eating M&Ms. The female kind—no nuts. Five hundred stomach crunches, two hundred push-ups. My feet are swollen."

Kyle put his naked feet up next to her. Her memory was so vivid, so controlled, it was as though Kyle was right there beside her in the booth plopping his feet into the platter of egg rolls. They were handsome feet. Strong and sleek. Pinkish, like monkfish filets she'd seen in the fish department showcase at Shop-Rite.

Tuesday hadn't been able to stop herself from reaching out to the feet, from rubbing them gently.

"Nice," Kyle had said. He had clasped his hands behind his head, cooing as her fingers pressed and stroked his heels and arches. "Take off my ankle support. I had a sprain last week, but it's okay now."

Tuesday slipped her fingers under the elastic cuff and wiggled the support slowly off Kyle's left foot. She had expected an athletic boy's foot to be callused, tight and gnarled with muscle and ligaments. Instead, this boy's were smooth as rayon and as forgiving as a hot water bottle.

"You have nice feet," Tuesday had said. Here in her replay, she took time to make every moment match the reality of the day before. She had deliberately let the ankle support drop onto her lap. She let her hands crawl down his foot, fondle the toes, and play piggly-wiggly with them. Toes with neither sweat nor slime nor lint.

"That feels great," Kyle had said.

"Thanks," Tuesday told him.

She looked into his eyes, and her breath quickened. Something stirred wildly in her blood and caught her private spotlight. She had never touched a boy so intimately before, no less had one smiling right at her with acknowledgment and pleasure and curiosity, eyes glaring at her beneath dangling clumps of lustrous midnight hair. She thought of sanctuaries and soaring cathedrals. Emotion burst from her chest, a hallucinatory rush that she was a living monstrance or elaborate dollhouse. She was a monstrance and his feet were the reliquary within. There in the booth at Madame Wu's, Tuesday was reexperiencing the pain and rapture and astonishment of touching Kyle. For the first time, life leapt up as an adventure. Existing was abruptly important and riveting, and she had to admit that she cared terribly, madly, for Maureen Willoughby's steady boyfriend.

"Pass the broccoli." Mrs. Racinski interrupted her daughter's reverie, without looking up.

Tuesday's mother sat like a squatting volcano juggling swollen squirt bottles of soy and sweet-and-sour sauces. She sprayed them on her heaping platter, rained them down onto lumpy mounds of white rice with flakes of scallion. Tuesday had put tiny, tiny portions on her own plate, but it was too late. Her small frame, like her mother's, had long ago been hidden under nearly two hundred pounds of clotted, hated fat. Tuesday made up deranged insults about herself. You're so fat, Tuesday, you're your own realm. You're so gross it'd take eighty days to go around you in a Lear jet. You're so enormous, Tuesday, you're a chip off the old, poor divorced volcano.

Mrs. Racinski slurped a jumbo stuffed oyster caked with water chestnuts into her mouth. She heard sounds. Now she looked up and saw the tears leaking down her daughter's cheeks.

"Tuesday? Are you *crying*? Are you? Is that what you're doing, dear? *Crying*?"

"No, Mom . . ."

"Well, you *look* like you're crying," her mother insisted. "Why are your eyes red? Have you been using my Lashes Galore again? Have you?"

"I didn't use much, Mother . . ."

"Dear, it's made from goat placentas. You're too young to need goat placentas. That mascara is very, very expensive. Major Hollywood stars use it. Lots of them."

"I know, Mom. And you have to work for it," Tuesday said. "I know how hard you work at Kmart—night after night—standing on your swollen ankles, your bunions hurting, killing you . . ."

"Yes, sweetheart," Mrs. Racinski said. She stared at Tuesday to make certain her daughter was being sincere. "But even if Lashes Galore grew on trees, it doesn't seem right to be a teenager and want suspensions of wet goat placentas on your eyes, dear. Does it?"

"I won't use it again."

"So expensive, and if it makes you cry . . ."

There were crunching sounds and a burst of thick fluid shot from a corner of Mrs. Racinski's mouth. The juices trickled down and fell onto her aquamarine fringe blouse, her favorite, the one she'd ordered from the Home Shopping Network. It had CASINO on it spelled out in Day-Glo playing cards.

Tuesday dabbed at her eyes with a napkin. "I used too much mustard."

Mrs. Racinski thrust another crunchy oyster into her mouth. "You know how careful you have to be with Oriental mustard. I don't know why those Chinese can't make normal mustards. I mean, they're in America and they should make it the way Americans like it. It should be delicatessen style, like the mustard at Nathan's or at the Bagel and Lox Omelette Shoppe. Like normal mustards." She stopped to take a breath and loosened the front tie on her blouse. "I thought we'd stop at Charlotte's Parlour for dessert."

"I don't want to."

"Don't be silly," Mrs. Racinski said. "You love her ice cream. You love it more than I do. Remember last time they had the apricot-raisin and you wanted an extra scoop? Do you remember? You had the apricot-raisin with caramel and I had the rocky road—and the pretty server insisted on giving me a taste of the cherry-berry. Do you remember the homemade cherry-berry? And the malted milk shake. Oh, my. Oh."

After awhile, Tuesday's mother inspected the empty Tupperware containers in her purse. She was tickled pink that her daughter hadn't cleaned her plate for a change. One plastic container was for the pea pods and uneaten shrimp with lobster sauce, and the other was for the extra egg rolls and three spicy fish dumplings and ribs. She always enjoyed microwaving the leftovers during the late-night reruns of *Masterpiece Theater* and *When Movie Stunts Go Bad*. She filled another cylinder with a mixture of pork-fried rice and the shark fin soup, and rehearsed her little jokes for the Chinese waiter. She'd speak Hungarian to him. Just a few words, like "Hello" and "What a nice man you are" and "What happened to the cat?" Amusing, good-humored things like that. And when he was most confused, she'd get him to put two or three extra fortune cookies into her bag along with an extra portion of orange slices and pineapple chunks with toothpicks in them.

And lots of Lite Duck Sauce packets.

"Oh, fug," her mother said, waving her largest rectangle of Tupperware.

"What?"

"Look at that. There's dried kraut from last month when we went to The Wienerschnitzel Wald. I've got to rinse it out." Mrs. Racinski pounded the table with a fist, huffed and grunted, and shimmied out of the booth. "Remember, you had sauerbraten and I had the Black Forest blood sausages? Remember?"

Tuesday watched diners in the other booths stare at the behemoth form as it rocked toward the ladies' room. There was an explosion of giggles from the cheerleaders. In a moment, Tuesday realized that Maureen Willoughby was heading down the aisle. Quickly, Tuesday pulled her sleeve down to hide the ankle support she was stroking on her wrist.

"Hi, Tuesday," Maureen said gently. She didn't wait for a response. "Imagine seeing you again. I mean, I saw you with that sandwich in the lunchroom. It looked so-o-o-o good. A sky-high pastrami. And then you answered that question about Hiroshima in history class." Maureen leaned closer, like it was a secret. "You freaked out Mrs. Pendergast knowing that was a picture of a farmer and his cart who were vaporized at ground zero. Everyone was impressed how you knew that. It's so horrible about the United States vaporizing *anybody*."

"Yes . . ." Tuesday said.

"Kyle just never stops talking about you and your project, Electrotropism and Kissing whatchamacallits?"

"Gourami. Kissing Gourami fish."

"Exactly. I mean, that's how 'brill' you are. Anyone else would have picked striped bass or baby flounders or . . ."

"Kyle picked out the kissing gourami."

"But it was *your* idea to use the electricity, right?" Maureen's eyes widened like saucers. "Zap 'em and see what happens! Kyle says it's so neat working with you. He thinks you're brill, too.

Super brill." She reached her hand across and grabbed Tuesday's arm. "Kyle dragged me with him all the way from fifth-period gym to your poli sci class. He wouldn't rest until he knew what kind of tape and wire you needed, all that insulated stuff you're wrapping around that gizmo you're using."

"The transformer."

"Exactly. Kyle says you're awesome, like a Louis Pasteur and Robert Oppensteiner and Mademoiselle Curie all rolled into one." Maureen let go of Tuesday, thrust her hands upward through her hair, and let it fall like tinsel. "Kyle never stops talking about you and your experiment together! I mean, who would have ever thought of electrocuting fish!"

"We're not *electrocuting* them."

"Whatever. I ran into you so often at school today—and now we're both at Madame Wu's. You just must think I'm following you . . ."

"No, I—"

"But I'm so glad to see you," Maureen said, "because I need your help. Not only me, but the whole senior class." She got up and slid in next to Tuesday. "I don't know if you're aware of the fact that I'm head of the prom committee, although I guess you do know. I mean, everyone knows." She laughed.

"I voted for you," Tuesday admitted.

"Did you? Did you vote for me? God, Tuesday, that makes me happy."

Maureen threw her hands back up into her hair and clawed at her bangs to make certain they were splashed over her high, slightly balding forehead. "Well, that's what I was telling my friends. I said, we need a brill brain on our committee. I told them you'd help us with a theme for the senior prom. We need something catchy, like 'Night in Rio' or 'Ice Castles' but extra snappy."

Tuesday felt her nasal passages closing and switched to mouth breathing. "I don't know anything about prom themes," she said.

"Sure you do. Kyle told me you're always coming up with original and fab stuff. I mean, however you came up with the idea of sticking electrodes into a fish bowl and shocking *fish* . . ."

"We're using half a volt . . ."

Maureen took a deep breath. "Whatever. I'll stop over to your house later, okay? I'll just run some things by you."

"I don't think—"

"You'll get your name in the prom program, and Miss Gale's giving everybody two service credits. Besides, I certainly want to see those kissing gouramies. I want to see the place where you're doing all that experimenting. You've got Kyle really pumped up." Maureen smiled hugely, then bolted away from the booth. Mrs. Racinski lumbered back shaking her dripping Tupperware.

"Who was that?" Mrs. Racinski asked, as she slid back into her seat.

"A friend," Tuesday said.

Her mother burped. "She'd be a very pretty girl if her legs weren't so short. She has very short legs, don't you think, dear?"

Mrs. Racinski finished packing up. It was as they were going out the door that Tuesday couldn't resist broadcasting her thoughts again. *Fall, little centipede. Fall now. Drop smack onto Maureen Willoughby. Land in Maureen Willoughby's hair or on her neck or her ears. Make her forget about me and prom themes. Make her forget about coming to my house . . .*

Outside, she and her mother heard the commotion. Quickly, Tuesday glanced back in through the cluttered win-

dows of Madame Wu's and past a sparkling BUDWEISER water-
fall sign. She glimpsed the screaming cheerleaders springing
from their booth. Maureen's arms flailed wildly, smacking at
her hair like it was aflame. What she was after fell to the floor,
and her friends hurled books and backpacks down at it.
Maureen herself grabbed a chopstick from the table. She
stooped swiftly—athletically—and began violently trying to
skewer something fleeing for the walls.

Escape and hide, centipedie, Tuesday broadcasted. *Give her the slip,
little bug.*

Tuesday walked her mother to the time clock at Kmart, kissed
her good-bye, and then headed home alone. She threaded her
arm through the handles of the plastic shopping bag full of leftovers, and pulled the ankle support down below the sleeve of her
frayed flannel shirt. She stroked the support tenderly and thought
of Kyle, his electric dark eyes and spellbinding feet. She began to
hum as her fingers traced his crude initials, a *K* and *E,* that had
been boldly branded in indelible camp-pen ink. The stretchable
shaft of the support shone radiantly under the streetlights. On a
deserted corner of Copperleaf Terrace and Death Hill Road, she
lifted the initials to her face, sniffed the support like a fine wine,
and clandestinely kissed it.

Tuesday turned up the walk to her house and picked up some
of the larger pieces of clay and plastic flowerpots left from the
time her mother had planted plum tomatoes in the front yard. A
rotting plywood wishing well sat in the middle of the lawn. Its
shingled roof now served as a feeding platform for crows. There
was a single leg bone left from a twenty-eight-pound turkey car-
cass Mrs. Racinski had put out weeks after Thanksgiving. To the
horror of neighbors, it sat there rotting for a month until a skunk

appeared one day at high noon and dragged the rib cage across the street and into a thicket behind the Our Mother Star of the Hill parish house.

Inside, Tuesday decided to broadcast aloud to the centipedes. "Hello, bugs. I'm back." She saw three of the larger, furrier centipedes staring at her from atop the Black & Decker microwave oven. She put the Tupperware in the refrigerator chiller. "If somebody comes over, I don't want you coming out, centipedies. Lay low or Maureen Willoughby will spray Raid and hydrochloric acid on you, and throw cosmetology books, and try to stick you with knives."

More centipedes, some four and five inches long, rippled over the ceiling-high piles of yellowing newspapers and magazines in the living room. Tuesday dragged several of the crumpled and ancient U-Haul boxes into the shadows of her mother's bedroom. She wiggled a dozen stacks of bound *National Geographics* and mildewed *Reader's Digest Condensed Books* against the walls to widen the path to the cellar door.

Finally, she attacked the stench of the house. That she had down to a routine. She sprinkled Wizard Love My Carpet on each of the open areas of stained shaggy rug, sprayed Lemon Pledge on the ceilings and doors, and mopped the kitchen floor with a green mixture of Mr. Clean and ammonia. She was about to feed her pets when the front doorbell rang.

Tuesday opened the door.

Maureen was silhouetted by a stark halogen streetlight. Her hair framed her face like a set of perfect blond parentheses. "It's me again," Maureen said, clomping into the living room in platform Doc Martens. She sniffed at the air, rotating her head like a radar disc.

"Jeez, what a lot of stuff."

"My mom doesn't like to throw anything out," Tuesday said, her voice shaking and growing small.

Maureen sucked in air, then started firing like a machine gun. "Did you come up with a smart prom theme yet? Did you? The entire squad is thrilled you're going to work on it. Jessica DeForest thought of 'Pirate Island.' We could make the gym into a ship and couples could drink out of hurricane lamps, and dance the plank. Letticia Goldman came up with 'Aliens' Adventures in Wonderland,' where you go in through a crepe-paper spaceship and everybody plays touchy-feely games, and we have Johnny D'Ambrosia deejay with alternative and techno music—and the cooking class can make cookies that look like Sigourney Weaver."

"I didn't get a chance to think," Tuesday said. "I was going to feed my pets."

"Oh?" Maureen said. "What kind do you have? My aunt has a Pomeranian and a shih tzu."

"I have a turtle and a ferret," Tuesday said, heading into the kitchen. "Garibaldi Rasputin—that's the turtle—he only eats grubs. They're in the refrigerator."

"Nasty," Maureen said, following into the kitchen. She planted her feet and stared at the piles of towels, dishes, and sheet-covered boxes that rose about her like Australian termite mounds. "I mean, grubs are larvae, aren't they? Worm things. Don't they crawl into the roast beef and bean sprouts?"

"Just once."

Tuesday grabbed a handful of grubs from the chiller and led the way to the turtle's tank in her bedroom. "'Aliens' Adventures in Wonderland' sounds interesting," Tuesday went on halfheartedly as she lifted the turtle off of its heat rock.

Garibaldi Rasputin was the size of her palm, and his head popped out like a Jack-in-the-box to nosh on the grubs.

"Yeah," Maureen said, "but I'll bet you're going to come up with something that's a lot more exciting. I'll bet it will be *romantic,* like 'An Evening in Venice' or 'Paris Escapade.'" She moved closer to Tuesday, backing her against the bed. "You just take a load off your feet and think," Maureen clarified. "I'll take care of Garibaldi."

Tuesday sat slowly down on the bed as Maureen's thin blue lips broke into a generous smile. She took the turtle from her. "You just chill," Maureen insisted. "Where's the crapper?"

Tuesday pointed toward the hallway.

"Nice. Your turtle can keep me company."

"I think you should put him back in his tank. He likes his heat rock."

"Oh, I bet."

Maureen carried the turtle into the bathroom and shut the door. Tuesday wanted to say, "No, no, you can't take Garibaldi Rasputin. You put the turtle back where he belongs. He doesn't belong in the bathroom."

But she didn't. All she did was begin to slightly shake, as though she were very cold. For a while, she tried to think of something creative, but she found herself sliding her fingers under her sleeve and stroking the ankle support. The touch of it made memories of Kyle flood over her once more. Fantasies began to flash though her mind—crazy things, like a vision of her swimming with him and a school of seals. And a dream of holding hands with him as the two of them toured a tea plantation. And dirt biking together in Sri Lanka. Zany, potent fantasies that he was letting her touch him again.

Tuesday cringed when she heard the toilet flush. She withdrew her fingers from the ankle support, and pulled her sleeve down as Maureen marched back into the bedroom without Garibaldi Rasputin.

"Where's my turtle?" Tuesday asked.

Maureen laughed. "Don't worry. Garibaldi's having the time of his life."

Tuesday moved to get up off of the bed. "I'd better get him."

Maureen clamped a hand on Tuesday's shoulder and pressed her back down. "Whoa. He's enjoying his grubs. He thinks he's at the beach. Loves those tiles. He was munching away on those larvae, making so much noise I told him to pipe down. 'Just pipe down,' I told him." She glared at Tuesday. "Did you ever have to tell him to *pipe down*?" Maureen didn't wait for an answer. She sat on the bed next to Tuesday and held both her hands. "We'll just stay together and you can tell me what really brill theme you've come up with."

Tuesday forced herself to speak. "I haven't thought of anything," she said, her voice practically disappearing. There was a clicking sound from the far side of the bed. Maureen dropped Tuesday's hands, and scooted around the bed to a wire habitat cage with a small black-and-white animal racing on an exercise wheel. "You sleep with your ferret, too? Oh, he's a real cutie."

"It's a she," Tuesday said softly. "She's smart."

"Does she bite?"

"No. You can ask her to run up your arm and kiss your ear, and she runs up your arm and—"

"What's her name?"

"Helen."

"Helen Ferret. Baby Jesus, what a neat name for a ferret."

Maureen stooped down next to the cage and opened the door. She thrust her hand in and grasped Helen firmly by the back of the neck. "So she's a smoocher. What a cutie, teeny-weeny ear smoocher." She stood up and spun around clutching the ferret.

"Please be careful with her."

"Don't worry about it."

"She's old . . ."

"Yeah? You must love her a lot then. Really love Helen Ferret. Helen, you cutie-pie-honey-bun-ear-smoocher." Maureen glared at Tuesday. "You stay on that bed until you come up with something respectable!" Maureen ordered. "Helen is going to help pick me out something to drink in the kitchen. You have a microwave?"

"Yes, but—"

"Well, I want a snack."

"I'll make you something. Helen doesn't like to be out of her cage."

"You have *cocoa*?"

"Yes."

"Great. I'll microwave me some cocoa, then. That'll just hit the spot." Maureen clutched Helen tighter. "You don't move off that bed, Tuesday. You just think. You think about everything." Maureen's face exploded into another huge smile as she turned and stomped down the hallway.

Tuesday's hands fell to her side. She'd begun to make low wheezing sounds as she slipped her fingers back onto the ankle support. She wanted to call out: PLEASE DON'T HURT HELEN. PLEASE. SHE'S A WONDERFUL GIRL. SHE'S A GOOD GIRL. SHE LOVES ME. SHE'S ALWAYS LOVED ME. SHE'S A

VERY GOOD GIRL AND SHE WOULDN'T HURT ANYONE.

Words wouldn't come out. Tuesday told herself it was because her mind was thinking about too many things at one time. It was worried about Garibaldi Rasputin. And it was afraid that Kyle had told Maureen about. . . . Well, there were things he could have told her. He could have even made things up, told her anything he wanted to. He could have told Maureen things just to make her jealous.

Her chest began to tremble.

A quaking.

There was a sound from the kitchen. The opening and closing of a small metal and glass door. Then the familiar *whoosing* sound of the microwave oven springing to life. Moments later Tuesday heard the first muted whimpering. A pathetic kind of groan that rose in volume until it became a shrill, ear splitting scream. Finally, it was a horrible, horrible shriek and Tuesday felt faint. There, on the bed, she began to cry and scream herself—but she couldn't move.

There was a muffled, small explosion, and then the shrieking stopped suddenly. The microwave cycle ended with a cheerful bell and the sickening, burning odor of fur drifted in to sting Tuesday's nostrils.

"Helen . . ." Tuesday fought to breathe.

Maureen came back into the bedroom. "Helen Ferret is very comfortable. I changed my mind about cocoa, but I found a nice, warm place for Helen." Maureen's head switched back into its radar mode. "Where's the gouramies? I want to see those gouramies now. Kyle said you were doing all your experimenting with him in the cellar, so show me. Show me the cellar."

Maureen pulled Tuesday to her feet and pushed her down the

hallway in front of her. "Hey, did you come up with a great prom theme yet? Did you?" Tuesday still couldn't speak. "What do you think of a one-word theme?" Maureen pressed on. She opened the cellar door herself and switched on the lights. "Wouldn't that be great? Easy to remember! A single word that would say it all. A catchy single word—like *Feet!*"

Tuesday fought to find her voice. "Maureen—"

"Isn't *Feet* a great theme for a prom?"

"I—"

"Wouldn't *Feet* be swell?"

Maureen locked an arm around Tuesday's waist and started down the stairs with her. Below, in the cave of a cellar, the fifty-gallon aquarium glowed with an eerie blue light. An electric train transformer sat smack in front of it, its wires hooked up to a pair of copper electrodes that were thrust deep into the ends of the shining rectangle.

"Oh, this is so neat," Maureen said.

As they approached the aquarium, a pair of kissing gourami rose to the surface. They were as big as children's hands, albino white with diaphanous ghostly tails. Their mouths kept opening and closing, a genetic reflex that made them appear to be perpetually drowning.

Tuesday stood frozen, feeling as though her mind were being wrapped in cellophane. Maureen talked to her as though she was talking to a deaf person. "WHAT DO YOU THINK? OF *FEET*? SEE, WE COULD DECORATE THE GYM LIKE A GIANT FOOT. COUPLES COULD ENTER THROUGH A DOOR CURTAINED WITH SHOELACES. THEY COULD DRINK OUT OF LITTLE PLASTIC SHOES, AND WE'D HAVE A DANCE MARATHON. AND A FOOT RAFFLE. ALL THE

GIRLS WHO WON COULD RUB ANY BOY'S FEET THEY
WANTED TO. WOULDN'T THAT BE FUN, TUESDAY? YOU
COULD RUB ANY BOY'S FEET!"

Tuesday thought of Helen and Garibaldi Rasputin and began
to weep.

"Turn on the transformer," Maureen commanded. She traced
the maze of wires to a fat black cord switch, flicked it on, and a
small green light glowed above the transformer's dial. Maureen
leaned closer to read the numbers. "You're right! It's set to half a
volt," she said as she grabbed Tuesday's hand and pressed it onto
the transformer dial. "More juice," she said. "These fish need
more juice. Turn it up!" Maureen roared. "Up!"

"Please, don't do this," Tuesday begged.

"Higher."

Maureen pressed Tuesday's hand firmly now, leaning on it so
the knob began to cut into her palm. She forced the dial upward.

Three volts! Five volts! Twelve volts!

Tuesday lifted her glance above the aquarium as gases began
to ripple up from the electrodes like bubbles in a soda. Another
movement had caught her eye. A motion of tiny yellow faces
staring at her from the stacks of rotting *TV Guide*s and piles of
fractured wicker baskets. Little bug heads swiveling on long, thin,
and furry bodies.

Maureen spotted the ankle support on Tuesday's wrist, and dug
her nails into it, tearing at it. Tuesday was aware of Maureen rep-
rimanding her now, hurting her right hand as she thrust it high
into the air.

"WHAT ARE YOU DOING WITH *THIS*?" Maureen shrieked.
"WHAT?"

Maureen twisted Kyle's initials on the support, distorting them fiercely as though they were images in a fun-house mirror. Tuesday began to breathe deeply. She felt her eyes convulse up into her head leaving only the whites exposed. When her eyes came back down, her lips stretched taut in a silent scream. Her hands lowered as though to pray, but instead, they surrounded the insulated case of the transformer. The voltage was so high now that sparks leapt across its two shiny steel terminals like the crackling Telsa coils of Frankenstein.

Suddenly, Tuesday's scream became manifest and she lifted the box with the speed and force of a catapult. The transformer flew upward, higher, higher, until it struck Maureen in her throat. The electric current flashed around Maureen's neck like a ring of lightning, and her body shook with huge, violent spasms, then drifted slowly to the floor. Tuesday watched Maureen's body twitching—vomiting!—coughing. She saw her beginning to crawl, but there came other sounds. In Tuesday's brain it was the roar of a locomotive, a sense that a great subway was hurtling beneath the cellar floor. The reality was a rustling as streams of small, absurdly footed creatures dashed from the stacks of foul newspapers and dank cellar drains. A wash of insects flowed up from a cement sink and out of cracks in a lard trap. Together, the bugs wove into a living, murmuring blanket.

Centipedes dropped from the ceiling, too—and onto Maureen's back and arms. The main wave didn't reach her until she had crawled as far as the first step of the cellar stairs, but then it began to crawl over her. The insects reached her face and raced up into her nose and down into the channels of her ears. They flooded her hair, bulging it, shaking it from within like it was a wig crudely attached to her scalp. Maureen cried out, and the swarm bathed her mouth, hundreds of long, angry insects rippling across her moist tongue and pouring down her throat.

The centipedes took control of Maureen's body as she lay coughing. Choking. Drowning in the furry tide. Tuesday watched her a while longer, then, finally, broadcast again.

Enough, she thought.

Enough.

Slowly—reluctantly—the horde of centipedes began to recede. It became a sluggish drift, swirling in lazy whirlpools and then slinking back down into the drains. As Maureen lay unconscious, a single set of filaments was left protruding from her nose, a pair of antennae waving, circling in the air. After another moment, the last mucus-covered centipede dashed from the nostril and disappeared into the cellar darkness.

I'll call someone, Tuesday thought. Authorities. Someone responsible and official. No matter what Maureen told anyone, Tuesday would say she was insane. Mad. That the cheerleader had fallen. She was showing off, doing wild and athletic and dangerous cheers in the cellar, and she tripped and hit her head. She hit her head and became delirious and feverish and even said she had had the flu. Even Kyle would think Maureen was lying. That she had hallucinated. Kyle who had said things he shouldn't have said. Kyle who was so consecrated that Tuesday knew she would forgive him anything.

Tuesday slid the ankle support back onto her wrist and stroked it smooth. Centipedes, she thought, as she stepped over Maureen and started up the stairs. They're like love. The way love had to come for her. Scary. Complicated. A powerful thing creeping from the shadows. For her, it had to come slowly. Love on tiptoe and with a hundred tiny feet.

Glorious little feet.

Paul Zindel on censorship

Ever since I began to tell stories there was always some group or person who wanted to censor me. I think most art is intrinsically that which arouses a degree of censorship: Something that is just the other side of what passes for the current decency and holds the ability to shock for a while. It started with my censoring myself, wanting to hide who I might be, and not having the courage to announce what my feelings and visions were about the awesome, often taboo mysteries of human love and intimacy. My father censored pieces of who I could have been, in a sense, because he fled the family when I was two. My mother wanted to censor anything, oral or written, that would reveal too many secrets about our strange, emotionally dwarfed family. As I became a professional writer, editors helped me obscure a darkness from my first drafts and balance it with laser bursts of compassion and understanding. With my very first book, *The Pigman,* I continued self-censoring by refusing to use invectives, and I rarely have (except for an experiment with one book called *I Never Loved Your Mind*). It came as a bit of a shock to me when one librarian in the New York City system said she would quit her job if forced to have *The Pigman* on her branch shelves. Her gutsy New York supervisors told her to go ahead and pack up, because young people were definitely going to have my book available to them.

I think I discovered, as my career moved along, that I was for the most part a very decent fellow. What was shocking about my work had much more to do with ideas than individual words. For a long time I ignored censorship as an issue for me because I believed the small amount of controversy I evoked was fashionable. I have since been exposed to more rabid confrontations involving what I would call "The CensorKooks." As odd as my adolescence and life have been, in my zaniest nightmares I could not have imagined the rituals of some adults who have tried to inflict pure madness on schools and libraries. One woman in Pennsylvania some years ago wanted the word *green* removed from all schoolbooks because green was the color of the Devil. A gentleman in Cincinnati demanded that all vowels be blackened out from each and every library book, his reasoning being "If you can't pronounce it, you can't do it." Last year, by sheer coincidence, I heard a minister/politician on an El Paso radio station scream: "And what are they teaching in our schools? They are teaching *Catcher in the Rye*! *The Pigman*! And *Lord of the Flies*!—three of the filthiest books ever written!" Quickly it became clear that he hadn't read any of them.

How protected I am, I now think, by the undaunted teachers and librarians and booksellers who are on the front lines and face the extreme attacks of some of The CensorKooks. And what an excellent job they do of protecting me and so many other writers. Should any book I've written—*any creation of mine*—be censored? Sure. But where? And when? And how? When I'm called in to help take on a CensorKook, I first remind everyone that kids are often capable of guiding themselves away from unsuitable material. Next, I make certain that all parental rights to decide what books of mine their children can and cannot read are protected. A child's parents *should* be able to forbid their son or daughter from reading a book of mine or anybody else's. However, those same parents should have zero control over what everyone else's kids can read.

Of course, a whole unified network of teachers, librarians,

administrators, and parent groups already in place has always been the most powerful garlic to ward off the CensorKook vampires. And they are vampires. The CensorKooks tend to be frustrated, jilted sorts of individuals who aren't receiving enough applause, recognition, or social acceptance to feed their megalomania. Defying logic at all costs, they tend to insist upon elaborate, noisy dances for the media, to showboat, exhibit their vulgar cancan of catastrophic thinking. After a few days or weeks, their dance tends to wind down. They tire. Everyone comes to their senses and gets tired of watching and listening to them. That is when a compassionate, vital, and sane community can move swiftly to drive a stake through their hearts and, thank God, dispatch them.

*So we do a sort of inverse thing for each other: He pro-
vides me with the* whoosh *that makes the drag-ass parts of
living more worth it; and I provide him with the vacuum of
experience that allows him to still feel any* whoosh *at all.*

*If I ever get married, there's nobody but Pauly for best
man.*

However, if I ever kill a person, that person is also Pauly.

Lie, No Lie

by
Chris Lynch

They say that in there somewhere we're all a little of this and a little of that; both sides of everything existing at the same time inside the same guy. Opposites add up to everything.

Like Pauly and me, right? We make no sense to anybody but ourselves. We are the wrong people for each other, nothing alike, but somehow we fill each other in and have done so for all of time—kindergarten, grade school, now. Pauly completes me, does the stuff I can't do, thinks the thoughts I'd never think, brings *action* to my life that I'd miss without him.

If it were not for Pauly, I wouldn't know what it was like to dive into the quarry.

If it were not for Pauly, I wouldn't know what a worm tastes like.

If it were not for Pauly, I wouldn't know that I am smart. I know because he tells me, and because he shows me that he is not.

So we do a sort of inverse thing for each other: He provides me with the *whoosh* that makes the drag-ass parts of living more worth it; and I provide him with the vacuum of experience that allows him to still feel any *whoosh* at all.

If I ever get married, there's nobody but Pauly for best man.

However, if I ever kill a person, that person is also Pauly.

* * *

Valentine's Day.

Pauly's thinking. He's always thinking, but especially on holidays, he's thinking.

"You thinkin' what I'm thinkin'?" he asks me over the phone. It's Saturday. It's Valentine's, and it's Saturday.

"Pauly, I'm never thinkin' what you're thinkin'. Nobody's ever thinkin' what you're thinkin'."

"Okay," he concedes. "I'm thinkin' let's go work out."

"See what I mean?" I tell him. "How would I ever have guessed that—that Valentine's means working out?"

"Proves you don't know me," he says. He's serious, and he's disappointed, because here we are all the way up to junior year together, so if I don't know the boy then who does? And if after logging this much time at it *I* still don't know him then how is anybody anywhere going to know him ever? Something for a guy to worry about, I guess; but if I didn't know him then I wouldn't know he's thinking this. And he is.

"Be ready in fifteen minutes," Pauly tells me.

I am ready in fifteen minutes. Pauly picks me up in forty, beeping the embarrassingly hick-sounding horn of his old red Ford pickup. There is somebody I don't know riding in the bed. I nod. He nods.

"Who's he and where are we going?" I ask when I'm inside and the rear wheels are kicking up gravel.

"Who's who?" Pauly asks.

I point out the small sliding window behind our heads. "Him. The person rolling all over the place in the back of your truck." And he is; he's flopping around madly, with the way Pauly drives. The guy tries to get himself a seat up on the wheel well. Pauly nails a frost heave and the guy is sprawling again.

"Oh," Pauly says, turning around to see. "Shit if I don't know. I never seen him before."

"Lie," I say.

"No lie," he says. Which doesn't mean that he's not lying, but it doesn't mean that he is, either. It doesn't mean anything, is what it means.

"Okay, so you don't know this guy. Is he going with us to work out?"

"I don't know. Better check." Pauly slides the little window. "You wanna go work out?"

"Ya," the guy says.

Pauly slides the window closed. "Nah, he's not going."

I don't bite. Pauly's in one of those moods. When he is, it's smartest not to bite.

"So where are we going to work out, Pauly?"

"Really nice new club down in Blue Falls. My brother Henry told me about it."

"You don't have a brother Henry. You don't have a brother at all."

"Do so. I just don't mention him much because he's the family embarrassment."

"Lie."

"No lie."

The small window slides open. "I'm Leon," Leon says, sticking his hand into the cab for me to shake.

"Hey," I say and I go to shake his hand but Pauly accelerates. Leon and his hand get sucked backward out of view.

"Why'd ya do that?" I ask.

"Because I'm jealous," Pauly says. "You belong to me."

I do a whole-body shiver. "Cut it out, Pauly. You know it makes me nervous when you say that stuff."

"That's why I say it. Your anxiety is always such a rush to those of us around you."

"You're welcome," I say as we pull into the parking lot of the gym.

The place looks more like a country music club than a health spa. It's two turns off the main road, carved out of thick woods, in a nowhere section of a suburb of nowhere. The building is a large wooden barn-shaped structure with a great big front wall but only a little bitty front door with an even bittier neon sign above it that reads simply The Club.

"Don't look like much, does it," says Leon, coming up from behind as we stand sizing the place up.

"Ya, but looks don't count. It's a lot of much inside," Pauly says.

"Thanks for the lift," Leon says, but doesn't make like he's going anywhere.

So Pauly and I leave him there in the lot among the four other cars that were there ahead of us.

"How'd you find this place, Pauly?" I ask as we approach the entrance.

"Leon told me about it."

"*Leon?*" I ask, forgetting the important rule. The important rule is not to sound too stunned by anything Pauly says, or he just gets all excited and goes on confounding you instead of answering your questions. "The guy in the truck, Leon? You know him? How do you know him?"

"Met him," Pauly says coolly, holding the door open for me.

"Met him where?"

"Met him at another club. You haven't been to that one, either."

"Forget I asked," I say. It's something I say to him a lot.

*   *   *

"You a member?" the front desk attendant asks Pauly. He's a big guy, but with those big buff shiny useless muscles you get from a health club.

"No, I'm not a member," Pauly says. "But my friend here is."

I cut in before he gets us in trouble. You have to be always ready to do that with Pauly. "No," I say to the attendant. "I'm not a member. But I could be. If it's any good, I might become a member."

"Oh good," the guy says, as if he gives a damn whether or not I join. "Then you can try us out for half the day rate as a prospective member. Five bucks."

"Cool," I say.

Pauly snorts a laugh. At me, or maybe at the guy.

"And you?" the attendant asks Pauly. "You interested in becoming a member?"

"Hell no," Pauly says.

"Ten bucks," the guy says, putting two locker keys and two black-and-white checked towels up on the counter.

I follow Pauly through the door, down a short corridor past the men's toilet, past two curtained dressing rooms, and into the main locker room. There are a few guys undressing at different locations; two sweaty ones who are on the way out, one dry one just arriving, like us. As we pass one sweaty one Pauly nods and points.

"Nice hog, dude," he says.

"Thanks," the dude responds as if they were talking about his car.

I gasp. I try to speak to Pauly, but only gasp again. When we do reach our lockers, I grab him by the back of the shirt. He's opening the locker, on his merry way.

"What?" he says to me. "What? Something wrong?"

"What kind of a milk dud are you?" I say. "You don't say that kind of thing to a guy. To a *naked* guy, in a locker room of a men's gym."

"Well, duh, Oakley," he says to me and proceeds to put stuff in his locker. "I couldn't very well say it if he was dressed. If he had his clothes on, how would I know what his hog looked like?"

"Shhhh!" I whisper, urgently. I glance over my shoulder to see if anybody caught that. They all did, since they are staring at us. "Would you stop saying that stuff? *Jeez.*"

"Why?" Pauly wants to know.

"Don't play this shit with me, Pauly. I hate it when you play this."

"Play what?" He has now slithered out of the shirt while I am still clutching it. He's pulling down his jeans.

"Pretending you're stupid. You know you're not supposed to talk about it."

"About what? About a guy's hog?"

"*Jesus,* Pauly," I say.

"No, Oak, I really don't get it. Why can't we say 'nice hog.' I mean, jeez, did you *see* the damn thing? *Somebody* ought to stand up and say something to the guy, if not applaud."

"No," I insist, "I did not see it."

"Lie," he says.

"No lie," I say.

"Then you ought to get yourself a guide dog, because that thing was a sapling and a half."

"Nevermind," I say. "The point is, you're not supposed to notice—even if you do. And nobody talks about it. I don't care if he's got one growing out of his damn forehead, you just say 'nice hat,' and leave it at that."

"Fine," he says. "I'll try not to make you nervous anymore if it's such a problem for you. I didn't know you were so hung up . . ."

"I am not . . ."

I am already so far behind in this discussion that Pauly doesn't even stay to finish it with me. He is in his sweats and on his way up to the weight room before I even have my shirt off.

"See you upstairs," he says, leaving me alone to dress. I hurry.

By the time I get up there, Pauly is drenched in sweat.

"How did you do that in only five minutes?" I ask.

"Intensity," he says with a knowing wink, "and a cup of water I poured over my head. I like to get that just-finished-a-marathon look right away."

I look away from sweat boy to size up the facility. The sizing doesn't take too long. There are two treadmills, one Stairmaster, one ergonomic rower, one heavy bag, six ancient Nautilus machines, and a huge mess of free weights spread all over the floor in front of the rack and the full-wall mirror. There is even one of what I believe were called "medicine balls" a century ago when anybody used them.

"Not exactly state of the art," I say.

"You don't even know what you're looking at," he responds. "It's all in what you *do* with the equipment that makes the difference. Here, let's play catch."

He, of course, is referring to the medicine ball. "With that? You're joking."

"No way." Pauly picks the ball up, bending at the knees and hoisting like he's power lifting a ton. Then he brings it up to his chest, walks six paces backward, and launches the thing at me.

It looks, from my angle, like a meteor coming down out of the sky to wipe me out. And to make it worse, the sight of it in the mirror off to my right pulls my eye just ever so slightly but enough . . .

I am flat. My back is pasted to the floor, and the ball is pasted to my shattered ribs.

"Oh, they are not shattered," Pauly says, laughing from high above me. He is not helping me up. He is not even removing the weight from my chest.

"Yes they are," I insist. "I can't even breathe. When I do—owwwww—my whole left side screams."

"Then just breathe with the other lung for now."

There is no one else in the gym, thank god, since this is quite embarrassing. But I am not going to beg Pauly to unpin me. I maintain my dignity; lie there suffering silently.

He's a sport, though. He kicks the medicine ball off me, gives me a minute for my lungs to reinflate, then offers me a hand.

Soon as I'm up, Pauly goes over and starts pounding on the heavy bag while I hobble off to the treadmill. I run ten steps before grabbing my side and stopping.

"I can't go anymore, Pauly," I say.

He stops. "Jesus, are you out of shape. You better become a member."

"Why, so I can come here all the time and have boulders thrown at me?"

"There's a lot more to the place than this."

"It stinks in here, too."

"Of course it stinks. It's a men's gym, it's supposed to stink."

"It's not a stink I've ever smelled before."

"Maybe you're just not man enough yet."

"Maybe not. I'm getting out of here, Pauly." I head for the door, and Pauly catches up with me.

"Wait," he says. "Let's just do something else. Let's go down to the pool for some laps."

"They have a pool?"

"Ya. Wanna go?"

"No."

"They also have steam and sauna, and a whirlpool. Hey, that's it, sit in the whirlpool, soak your bruised ribs."

"Broken."

"Fine, soak your broken ribs."

This I like. I follow Pauly through a maze of corridors, past the glass wall of the pool area, past the steam room, the sauna room, the cafe, the bar.

"For a place with such a crappy gym," I say, "they have some pretty decent extras here."

"Gotta have your priorities," Pauly says.

We are sitting in the Jacuzzi for ten minutes before I start to feel a little better. Then I start to feel a lot better. It is the hottest hot tub I have ever been in and I can hardly stand to stay in it but it is irresistible at the same time. The room is kept cooler than the rest of the building, making the hot tub feel all that much stronger, the steam rising off the water's surface and rolling back over my exposed face. I cannot feel my ribs at all anymore. I cannot feel anything at all from the neck down, and I love it. I am a floating head, looking across at Pauly's floating head with his eyes closed.

Until a person, naked, with a checkered towel over his shoulder, passes through the room without a word—in one door, out the other.

"Pauly," I say, as he seems to have slept through it. "Pauly, a naked guy just walked through."

"Ya?" sleepy-eyed Pauly says. "Was it the guy with the hog? You should have woke me."

"No, it wasn't him. I think it was that guy Leon."

"Oh," Pauly says, and tries to go back to sleep.

"Pauly," I snap and get right to my feet. The blood zooms to my head. Everything goes black, and I sit back down before I fall. "Pauly, is it all right to just be walking around like, naked, all over the place?"

Pauly shrugs while keeping his eyes closed. "This is a very relaxed joint," he says calmly. "Which is just the type of joint you need. Unclench, will ya, Oak?"

"And where is your brother Henry, anyway?"

"C'mon, Oakley, I got no brother Henry, you know that. God, you're such a rube."

I stand again, more slowly this time. "I want to go," I say. "I've had enough."

"What, we just got here practically. Take a steam."

"I don't wanna take a steam."

"They have an awesome steam here. They're famous for their steam. Take a steam."

"I don't want a steam, I told you."

Pauly is once again amused. Because I am nervous.

"You're right," he says. "We should take a sauna instead. I always preferred a sauna myself—better for the skin, I think—

and they are equally famous here for their sauna."

"I don't want to take a sauna, dammit, I want to go."

"But I ain't completely boiled yet," he says, raising one leg out of the water for me to see. He looks like a cooked shrimp, the leg all pink and veiny.

I am by now on my way anyway. I have my towel around my shoulders, my bathing suit dripping a trail behind me, as I make for the hallway. Already I am chilled to the bone.

"Fine," Pauly calls. "Just give me a couple more minutes, and I'll catch up."

The locker room has, on one wall, a row of shower heads lined up together like the ones in the school gym. There is one guy showering there when I come in, his back to me. There are also a group of separate stalls near the toilets, secluded in the farthest corner from the exit for the more modest among us. That would be me. I grab my soap and shampoo from my locker and head for a private.

They form their own little corridor, the individual showers, with four on the right and four on the left. There is a hook mounted on the tile wall outside each position. The second hook on my right and the third on the left each has a towel hanging from the hook. I can hear the water spraying hard. Good water pressure. I'm happy.

I walk the short walkway between showers. There are shower curtains hanging from brass rings over each position, but all eight are left open. I pass the blue towel and vaguely notice a figure in there but make sure not to look. I reach the third pair of stalls.

I really can't be blamed for looking. If you don't want to be looked at, you close the curtain. Casual is right. Maybe Pauly, too, is right. So fine then, I'm relaxing.

I'm staring.

It's the guy with the hog.

And ya, it's a lot. It's like—a lot. Something to talk about, if you were the type of guy to talk about stuff like that, which I'm not, as I've said. But then again I wasn't the type to stare at it either, a little while ago.

"Can I help you?" the guy says to me.

"Shit." I actually say it when I realize I have been frozen there staring at him. And I realize it's not even the original hog guy, but a new one. What am I, like, a browser now?

I rush away, head for the last stall, as far away from him, it, them, as possible. I throw on the water, make it as hot as possible. I hang my towel, break out the soap, and wash myself, scrub and boil and scale myself, as quickly and as thoroughly as I can. I am shivering slightly. I can see this, but cannot feel it because I am again as numb as I was in the hot tub.

Pauly is by now in the stall opposite me. Laughing, naturally. "What are you so worked up about?" he asks in a big whisper.

I whisper back. "Couldn't they even pull the curtains, for god's sake?"

Pauly laughs. "That wouldn't help. Look." He pulls his own shower curtain closed, pressing it to his naked body.

Not only is the curtain material transparent, it actually works like a magnifying glass, distorting and enlarging.

Pauly pops his head around the curtain, looks down at himself. "I gotta get some shorts made out of this stuff."

I am scrubbing so fast the steam coming off my body may actually be smoke. I grab the shampoo, lather up madly.

I don't have my eyes closed for more than ten seconds.

"Hi," he says, and he's right behind me. He is so close I can feel the thin buffer of air between us, like the wrong ends of two magnets, but he does not touch. I can't breathe, much less answer. The shampoo seeps down onto my face because I have stopped scrubbing.

"I'm Henry," he says.

He reaches around from behind, and he puts his hand on it.

I'm hard as a diamond. I don't want to be. I have no business being.

"I can explain that," I say, my voice quavering as I grab Henry's wrist and push it away.

"Not necessary, relax," he assures me. His manners are good, except for the way he keeps doing things without asking.

He places his hands on my shoulders and turns me toward him. I move in his grip. I do as directed.

Henry goes down on his knees, right there in the shower, with that hard water pressure slapping down on him. He's looking up at me like a dog begging. I'm thinking, *Excellent water pressure. Fantastic water pressure* . . .

"No," I say, and am very happy to hear myself say it. Because I don't feel in charge. I feel like I'm a spectator, watching to see what my next move is. I don't feel, here, now, like this body I'm in is mine. I look across to the other stall, to my friend to help me, and he's watching. He's watching, hard, he's watching.

Before I look back down, Henry's mouth is on me.

I open my own mouth to holler at him, but I don't holler at him.

I hesitate.

For three seconds, and about fifty thrusts of Henry's busy little skull, I don't do a thing.

"I said no," I say firmly, placing my hand on Henry's forehead and wedging him from me.

Henry rises to his feet. He is bigger than me, and older than me, but I am ready to do more than push him. I'm not a tough guy by anybody's measure, but I can do this, here and now.

"I don't see what you're so pissed off about," Henry says. "You're the one who hung your towel in Henry's stall. You knew this was Henry's stall. Everybody knows this is . . ." He looks away for a second, over to Pauly. "He knew, right?"

Pauly nods at Henry. The water remains hot. I go cold. I feel my fists opening and closing. One for Henry, one for Pauly.

"And look," Henry continues to explain to me why it is I actually did invite him. "Pert shampoo, even. You're flying all the flags."

"I like to have a little bounce in my hair, is that all right with you," I snort, and suddenly see myself there, primed for combat, naked, with a gay man, in the shower. This is such a classic Pauly setup. "Pert shampoo," I manage a nervous small laugh at Henry, who does smile back. I look over at Pauly.

Why isn't he laughing?

Henry pulls away and backs out of the shower. "Listen," he says, "you think I don't know? You think I don't understand? Don't worry, I'm not mad."

"And I'm not worried."

"I'll be in the bar upstairs, if you want to stop in for a glass of suds. On me."

Henry's a gamer, I'll say that.

I tell him I'll think about it. But I have no intention of thinking about it.

* * *

We're in the truck on the way back to Whitechurch. We ride all the way without talking about it. Pauly stays on the highway as we pass town. We keep going. We start talking finally.

"Shitty joke, Pauly," I say.

"No joke," he says.

"What was it then?"

"A favor. At least I thought."

"A favor? Pauly, if I wanted guys . . ."

"No, you wouldn't. You never would."

"Well, I don't anyway."

"No offense, Oakley, but really, would you even know?"

"I know, okay."

He laughs at me. Sometimes when Pauly laughs at me it makes me feel better because it reminds me that nothing is that big a deal. Pauly says that all the time, and he's right. But I forget a lot and one kind of laugh he does, reminds me.

This is the other kind.

I want to hurt him now.

"I fucked Lilly, is how I know." Lilly is my best friend. She's also Pauly's girlfriend. I wait for the reaction. I watch his face. I watch him run through the possibilities.

"Lie," he says.

"No lie," I say, and he knows it could well be true. He also knows that he has never done with Lilly what I say I've done with Lilly. He probably does not know that she told me. I will tell him that, too, some other time when I feel like hurting him again.

"You slept with my Lilly," he says slowly, nodding, driving. This time it is Pauly's test. He tests me all the time, and I almost never do it back. Now I'm doing it. Difference is, I feel bad already. I nearly apologize before he can respond, but . . .

"Next time can you let me know," he says, "so I can watch?"

He makes me smile. He makes himself smile. And like that, in his Pauly way, he has ended it There will be no escalation. No tit for tat, no pass-fail. No apologies. It's gone for now. Not the *stuff* that we've churned up, but the tension between him and me. Somehow it feels like we always wind up on the same side of whatever issue, even if the issue is us.

"My dad always told me," I say, after one more long pause, "to come tell him right away after I got my first hummer. To tell him how it was. *Now* what am I gonna tell him?"

Pauly grins widely, leans just slightly toward me. "Right, Oak, so . . . what *are* you gonna tell him? How'd it go? Huh?"

He's really, really, really interested in this answer.

I won't give him one. Instead I reach out and clap him on the shoulder. He pulls away violently.

"Hey, keep your hands off me, ya deviate."

He appears to mean it.

My first tangible experience with censorship came when my agent sent me a clipping from a law journal in which they were tracking challenges to books. And there I was, challenged in Texas for *Iceman*. My first thought was, Me? Come on guys, there must be some mistake. You got the wrong guy. But right beside me in the same article was Judy Blume being similarly challenged. Cool, thinks I, I'm hanging with a better class of undesirable these days.

But of course, cool it was not. Challenged. Challenged? It sunk in then, that people were challenging the right of my book to even exist. Not challenging me to a fistfight over something I'd said that offended, not challenging me to debate one fictional detail or another. In fact it was the opposite. They wanted to preclude any debate at all.

It came up again, in a subtler but even more disturbing way, when I wrote The He-Man Women Haters Club series. Before publication there was considerable pressure to change the title. Reports were coming back to me about people resisting the books because women-hating was not a particularly fashionable idea. Well, ah, yes, I knew that already. But it's all there in the book. It's about the *absurdity* of male posturing. It's about our being so uptight and essentially chickenhearted that we were not capable of saying we ever feared women (or feared anything, for that matter), so we had to say we hated them instead. It was about how men passed down this cockeyed legacy to boys.

I considered this my feminist series. No, really, I did.

Because it was lampooning machismo, not endorsing it. And if you read three pages in, you knew it. But a weird little back-

and-forth went on then: "Change the title and we will open the book," say they. "Open the book and you will appreciate the title," says I.

I felt like this episode had been scripted by Joseph Heller.

In the end the choice was mine, and the implications were made clear. The books might suffer if I didn't change the title. I thought about it. I have to confess that I did not automatically do the "righteous indignation" thing. I thought about it. I do hate to see any creature suffer, particularly if the creature was written by me.

But I couldn't do it. I had to believe that there was room for the writer to be a little bit risky in trying to get his message across with impact. And I figured, this is the kind of thing we are going to have to get used to dealing with, so we should have an overriding philosophy to guide us through.

I decided this will be mine: Challenge me? I challenge you back.

After watching him helplessly for several moments, Ben tore frantically out of the dorm. In a short time he had amassed everything he could remember anyone ever having suggested for a hangover: aspirin, sleeping pills, black coffee, and tomato juice. Michael, his head buried under the covers, refused all these remedies in a muffled and anguished tone. Finally, he allowed himself to be dragged from the bed, steered awkwardly downstairs, and taken on a walk around the campus. Hanging on to Ben's arm, he stumbled hesitantly forward. "I think we were in the bedroom together," he kept saying, trying to organize the disconnected images in his mind, "but I can't remember what happened." Ben told him not to worry about it.

Something Which Is Non-Existent

by
Norma Klein

The Music Room was nearly empty. Only one person remained besides the boy working the phonograph and Ben, who sat sprawled in a lumpy armchair, idly turning the pages of an essay on Gibbon. Pulling his jacket tighter, Ben glanced distractedly around the room, out the window, and then under the table where a mangy cat lay dozing complacently. In the opposite corner the other boy hunched over a book, his hair sharply illuminated by the intensified glare of a lamp just above his head. Suddenly he looked up, meeting Ben's stare. Ben quickly turned away, pretending to examine the record list. A few minutes later he glanced back. The boy's face, languid and pale, with thin austere features and heavy reddish hair drooping on its forehead reminded Ben of the faces on Greek coins. Although it was exciting to him in art, he mistrusted such beauty in people. He himself was short and stocky with dark eyes which peered inquisitively from behind thin, gold-rimmed glasses.

Abruptly, the boy got up, stuffed his book under his arm, and left the room. Ben, after hesitating a few moments, followed him. Outside the door he stopped to arrange his papers, his head throbbing from the sudden silence. Peering into adjacent rooms, he searched for the other boy, but could not find him.

In the cafeteria downstairs there was jovial off-key singing and the floor was damp with pools of beer; a party was being held with the local town girls. Although Ben had spent his own freshman year drinking rather heavily and occasionally taking up with various town girls, he had always done so rigidly, coldly, without enjoyment, and even now was disgusted when he saw others doing that sort of thing with wild enthusiasm. Probably because of this, he almost always spoke disparagingly of the social activities of the university, such as football games and fraternity initiations and, when they were mentioned in his presence, referred to them as "unhealthy displays of the herd instinct in man."

Unobtrusively, he crossed to the other side of the cafeteria where, although the lights were dimmed, he saw the boy sitting at the end of a long row of empty tables. Approaching the table with his cup of coffee, he asked, suddenly flushing with confusion, "May I join you?"

"Yes." The boy's voice was low. Ben sat down silently. There was a pause. "Did you like the piece they were playing?" the boy asked.

Ben, who did not remember the piece, answered hastily, "Yes," staring at the piece of lemon the boy was chewing on. He had never seen anyone eat lemon plain before, and it made his own lips pucker.

"What's the celebration for?" asked the boy, indicating the other end of the room.

Ben shrugged his shoulders. "Who knows? I think it's to celebrate a football game we won . . . or is the football season over?" He smiled at his own ignorance.

The boy smiled back. "I'm not much up on those things either," he said.

They both continued sipping their coffee in silence, like strangers, but when they were done, they walked back to the dorms together, and there sprang up between them a casually malicious conversation about the university, such as arises between people who feel they are in agreement and do not have to give explanation for their views.

A group of boys were singing and yelling at the end of the corridor as Ben stood alone in the yard. The boy, whose name was Michael, said that he would have invited Ben to his room, but that a friend of his was there with his girl. Again they smiled at each other. As Michael leaned over the staircase, the shadow of his profile stretched along the wall. Quickly, Ben sketched it in his pocket with the tip of his finger.

"You can come tomorrow, though," Michael said. "I'll meet you here."

From then on Ben always studied in Michael's room. Since Michael had a phonograph and records, there was no need to go to the Music Room. Ben was relieved to escape from its distracted bohemian atmosphere. In the spring he was especially glad since he did not have to cross the campus so frequently. After classes he hurried away, passing the girls who stood on the doorsteps in their pastel-flowered dresses, giggling and chatting. They frightened him, and he went by with his eyes down, his books clutched tightly under his arm.

In Michael's room he slouched comfortably on the bed with his socks and shoes off, the phonograph going full blast, chewing gum—a habit he disliked in other people and never did in public—and doing his work. At four o'clock Michael returned from his Modern Novel course, raving at the stupidity of the class and the teacher. The book they were reading was *Swann's Way* and, although Michael was reading it in French, whenever he went to class he left this edition in his room and carried an English one instead so people would not think he was a snob. Sitting down, he began to read with his big French dictionary. He chuckled to himself a few times and finally bounded up, saying, "You must listen to this! Just this one thing!" As he paced the room, he read aloud in French which Ben did not understand. "You get the difference, though?" he said eagerly. "You can tell by the sound, can't you? . . . 'Une heure n'est pas une heure,' " he crooned in a low melodic tone. " 'C'est une vase, rempli dos sous, des parfumes . . .' " Since it was a passage he liked, he typed it on a scrap of paper and Scotch-taped it on the wall beside several other assorted quotes. "All the greatest things we know have come to us from neurotics," read one. "It is they and they only who have founded religions and created great works of art."

Frequently he and Ben went to the cafeteria for coffee. It was usually crowded with teenagers dancing to jukebox music. The girls, strutting by with pert, flirtatious expressions, knocked accidentally into the table, blushed, and ran scurrying across to whisper with their friends. Ben and Michael sat in a corner, each sure that the other was too absorbed in their conversation to notice these distractions. Michael discussed his latest theory of literature, drank black coffee, and ate wedges of lemon. When they came back to the dorm again, it was nearly evening and, before they returned to their work, Michael quoted, "'For whatever moral reasons he may do it, the artist who gives up an hour's work for a conversation with a friend knows that he is sacrificing a reality for something which is non-existent.'"

Toward the end of April Michael began going out with a girl from his Modern Novel class. She was also reading Proust in French. Often they went to parties together. One evening he returned very drunk. Ben, who had been studying in his room, watched him collapse, grinning, in the middle of the floor and laugh with painful, uncontrollable hilarity for nearly five minutes. When the last gasps of mirth had subsided, he rose, walked quickly to the bathroom, threw up, and crawled silently back to bed where he lay on his back, heavy-lidded and pale, moaning to himself. After watching him helplessly for several moments, Ben tore frantically out of the dorm. In a short time he had amassed everything he could remember anyone ever having suggested for a hangover: aspirin, sleeping pills, black coffee, and tomato juice. Michael, his head buried under the covers, refused all these remedies in a muffled and anguished tone. Finally, he allowed himself to be dragged from the bed, steered awkwardly downstairs, and taken on a walk around the campus. Hanging on to Ben's arm, he stumbled hesitantly forward. "I think we were in the bedroom together," he kept saying, trying to organize the disconnected images in his mind, "but I can't remember what happened." Ben told him not to worry about it.

When they returned to the dorm, Michael staggered to the bed where he expired in a heap, one half of him hanging limply over the edge. Ben pushed him onto his back, pulled down the shades, and began to straighten up the room. Once, since it was dark, he tripped over a lamp cord. "Excuse me," he said spontaneously, then looked guiltily around the room, afraid he had awakened his friend. But Michael continued to sleep calmly, unaware of this or of any of the anonymous creaks, flutters, and rumbles that filtered into the silent room. Quietly, Ben covered him with a blanket and returned to his own room.

The next weekend was Spring Weekend. Ben watched the preparations for it with distaste: the banners in phosphorescent lettering hung over the cafeteria, the exclamatory editorials in the college newspaper, the torch-lit procession of paper floats, moist and wilted from the rain, winding through the streets of the local town, and, finally, the sight of Michael spending two hours getting dressed for the dance to which he was going with the girl in his Modern Novel class. By eight o'clock, with Ben's white silk scarf wrapped around his neck, in a tweed coat and black leather gloves lined with rabbit fur, he looked very distinguished. Even so, Ben told himself, he was glad it was not he who had to wear such an outfit and go to a dance. Michael had to wait for the girl to call him before he left to pick her up. For half an hour he paced the room, squinting critically at himself in the mirror, asking disconnected questions, and forgetting at once what he had asked. "She's not going to call," he said severely. "It's finished. I knew this would happen."

"Relax," said Ben placidly, looking up from his reading. "Don't worry about it so much."

When the girl called, Michael bounded out of the room, grinning foolishly. "See you later, alligator," he said.

Ben read steadily for three and a half hours, stopping only to add another sheet to his file of notes which he shuffled through with a pleasant sense of accomplishment, as though the thickness of the pile were physical evidence of his increase in wisdom over the year. At midnight, putting down his book, he prowled around the room, idly lifting up pencils and staring at Michael's quotes on the wall. Suddenly it occurred to him that it would have made no difference if he had spent all year going for hikes or even getting drunk as he had done as a freshman.

He felt as though it would matter little to him if he never finished Gibbon at all. Looking moodily at his stack of notes, he
imagined it burning to ashes along with all the outlines and
notes he had ever taken. It seemed to him that there should be
some logical reason why this, at least, should matter a great
deal, but he could not think of what it was.

Slipping on his sweater, he went outside and down by the
lake, puffing intensely on a cigarette. It was a warm night with
air so luxuriously sweet-smelling that Ben found it hard to
breathe. As he walked slowly down the path, he hummed a line
from Handel's *Water Music.* The lively, yet dignified tune cheered
him up. As he rounded the side of the lake, looking around with
pleasure at the dark water, he almost ran into a couple making
love on a blanket. He was so startled he cried out, but they didn't
notice. His heart pounding, he walked rapidly back to the main
road, stopping at the cafeteria to get some chewing gum.

Michael, sitting at one of the tables with the girl, stood up,
smiling cheerfully, and waved to Ben to come join them. With
difficulty, Ben edged his way through the crowded smoky
room. He straightened his sweater clumsily and stuffed the
package of gum in his pocket, ashamed of his nervousness.

When he got there, he stood with his hands in his pockets,
not looking at the girl. "Have a seat," said Michael heartily.

Ben sat down. On the table he saw two saucers, an apple core,
and the hands of the girl, round and pink. "How was the dance?"
he blurted out, feeling that the girl must be annoyed at his sloppy
clothes.

"Oh, it was—," they both began at once, stopped, looked at
each other, and laughed.

"Go on," said Michael.

"No, you go," said the girl, blushing.

"It was all right," said Michael, "as these things go."

"Many people there?" asked Ben.

"Yes. Quite a few," replied Michael. "It was pretty crowded."

Ben nodded. There was a pause. Michael yawned, and the girl, leaning forward, poked her finger playfully in his mouth. He snapped at it like a turtle with mock ferocity, and she drew back, giving a little cry. Ben wondered why he had come. Looking at the girl's face, he saw that her nose was shiny, and, for some reason, this annoyed him a great deal.

"Want some ice cream?" asked Michael.

Ben shook his head.

"You, Clara?"

"No," she said softly, looking at the table.

Michael smiled at Ben. "She's on a diet. Can you imagine?" he said, getting up from his chair.

Since Ben found the topic of women's diets singularly uninteresting, he said nothing.

Clara looked at him pleasantly. "That's my fatal weakness," she said. "I love sweet things—candy, gum, ice cream. Do you?"

"No," he replied shortly. "Not very much."

She toyed with a salt shaker. "You're lucky. I'm afraid I'm ruining my teeth."

For the next few minutes Ben and Clara sat silently, looking around the room. "That's a nice song they're playing," said Clara finally. "I think it's from *Carousel*. Or is it *Oklahoma*?"

As it happened, Ben knew the tune was from *Carousel* since he had recently heard someone mention it, but since he didn't want her to think he was someone who kept up to date on popular songs, he replied, "I don't know."

There was another pause, longer than the first. Again Clara broke the silence by saying something else which, because of the noise, Ben could not hear. "What?" he asked, pulling his chair closer.

"Are you also interested in . . ."

Although Ben missed the last word, he was too embarrassed to ask her to repeat it again. He nodded.

"What have you read by him?" Clara asked in a politely interested voice.

"I'm sorry," Ben said, feeling himself grow hot around the ears. "I missed what you said before. By who?"

"By Proust," said Clara, smiling just perceptibly.

"Oh . . . No, I haven't."

"What sort of things do you read?"

"Well, Gibbon . . . *The Decline and Fall*," he replied reluctantly, watching the glittering things on her dress and wondering what they were made of.

"How do you like it? I think I once had to read part of it for a history course, and by the end of the term I was about ready never to lay eyes on the thing again."

"Really?" said Ben. "I find it extremely interesting." He knew perfectly well that what she said was true, that he himself felt nearly the same way, but nevertheless he was irritated by her remark. Disparaging theories from Nietzsche about female intelligence occurred to him, and it seemed to him that her manner of speaking, the expression on her face, her eyes, everything about her reflected unthinking frivolity. As for Proust, why should he have read him? No one read Proust except people in advanced French classes, and even they only pretended to like it and were really bored silly all the way through.

When Michael returned, Ben stood up, saying impatiently, "I guess I better go."

"Oh sure. Back to the old grindstone," said Michael.

Ben did not look at him.

Clara touched his sleeve lightly. "Are you really sure you can't stay a little longer?" she asked.

"No, I really can't," said Ben, mimicking her slightly, and hurried out, thinking that such insincerity was grotesque.

When he reached the room, he walked around it a few times and finally stopped, staring at the wall. He thought, "It will never matter if I do anything again or not." Feeling profound, he typed a two-page treatise on the meaning of friendship, making a good many mistakes since he kept hitting the wrong key or else two keys at the same time. When it was finished, he took a warm bath, reading it aloud to himself, the paper puckering from his wet fingers. When he emerged, draped in a striped towel, he saw the boy from across the hall standing near the sink.

"You okay?" he asked. "I thought I heard you talking to yourself in there."

"Sure," said Ben. "I'm fine." He decided that what he had just written was the biggest piece of baloney he had ever read and returned to his room, chuckling to himself.

A Tribute to Norma Klein by Judy Blume

Norma Klein was my first friend who also wrote. We had a lot in common. We were born in the same year, our favorite childhood books were the "Betsy-Tacy" series, and each of us, as Norma put it, "rushed into reading adult novels at eleven or twelve, to find an alternative to the idealized, sanitized, sentimentalized books meant for readers our ages." For a short time, we even shared the same literary agent.

We met in the early seventies and bonded over tuna fish sandwiches at Schrafft's on our way to a meeting of children's book writers. I had read an advance copy of Norma's first book for children, *Mom, the Wolfman, and Me,* and was charmed by the characters and the story.

A few years later we found ourselves together on the "most censored list." Norma's work was banned because of her nontraditional families (in *Mom, the Wolf Man, and Me* the spirited protagonist is raised by a mother who has never married) and the fact that she accepted and often wrote about her young characters' sexuality.

Norma said, "I'm not a rebel, trying to stir things up just to be provocative. I'm doing it because I feel like writing about real life. I still can't believe there's anything objectionable about telling it like it is."

One of my favorites of her books is *Naomi in the Middle,* a warm story of a loving family with two small daughters. The mother is expecting a third child, and Naomi, the youngest, is concerned about being displaced. The illustrated book contains silly rhymes—"I'm going to China to see your vagina. / I'm going to

Venus to see your penis"—and a few sentences about how con-
ception occurs, both of which make it a favorite target of the censors. A couple of years ago I was on a panel discussing censorship
and *Naomi* when a woman in the audience stood up and asserted
the book should be banned because it promotes alcoholism. None
of the panel members had a clue what she was talking about. She
explained that on the night of the birth, when the father and
mother go to the hospital, the grandmother comes over to stay
with the two young sisters. After reassuring them that all will be
well, she fixes warm milk laced with rum, to help them get back
to sleep. "We don't want anyone telling our children it's okay to
use alcohol!" the woman in the audience shouted, proving when
it comes to censorship, if it's not one thing, it's another.

Norma knew writers who'd grown so discouraged, they'd
given up and left the field of children's books altogether, and
others who'd backed off to escape the fallout of the censors. But
she kept going full steam ahead, refusing to water down her children's books. She swore she never would. "I've never written
anything I wouldn't want my own daughters to read," she said.

Smart, feisty, and enormously talented, Norma was a prolific
writer, publishing one or two children's books almost every year,
plus a number of adult novels. The children's book world was
shocked when she died suddenly in 1989. She was fifty years old.
I miss her friendship. I miss her voice on the page. Sometimes I'll
take down one of her books and begin to read, just to hear her
again. There is no way I could have edited a book of stories by
censored writers without including Norma and I'm grateful to
her husband, Erwin Fleissner, for finding this one, written when
Norma was a student at Barnard College and originally published in the *Focus* literary journal in 1959. It shows her early

promise, her gift for creating believable, complicated characters, and her keen, observant eye.

If she were alive today, Norma would still be speaking out on the same issues, encouraging other writers to keep going, full steam ahead.

About the Contributors

Judy Blume is the author of some of the best-known and widely read novels ever published. More than 65 million copies of her books have been sold, and her work has been translated into twenty languages. She has won more than ninety awards and is a recipient of the American Library Association's Margaret A. Edwards Award for lifetime achievement. Judy is an active spokesperson for the National Coalition Against Censorship. She lives in Key West and New York City with her husband, George Cooper. Judy's web address is: www.judyblume.com

David Klass has written several award-winning novels for young adults, including: *Wrestling with Honor* (1989), which was named one of the 100 "Best of the Best" Books for Young Adult Readers of the last 25 years by the American Library Association; *California Blue* (1994), winner of the Keystone State Reading Association's 1996 Young Adult Book Award; and *Danger Zone* (1996), which was chosen the Outstanding Work of Fiction for Young Adults in 1997 by the Southern California Council on Literature for Children & Young People.

Klass also wrote the screenplays for *Kiss the Girls* (Paramount, 1997) and *Desperate Measures* (Mandalay, 1998). He lives in New York City.

Norma Klein endures as one of the best-known and most controversial authors of young adult fiction. She wrote thirty books for young adults, including *Mom, the Wolf-Man, and Me, Breaking Up, Love Is One of the Choices,* and *It's Okay if You Don't Love Me,* as well as numerous short stories. At least nine of her books have been banned or targeted for removal from library shelves. Following her death in 1989, the PEN/Norma Klein award was established by the PEN American Center to honor emerging voices in literature for young people.

Julius Lester is the author of twenty-nine books for children and adults, including *To Be a Slave* (Newbery Honor Book), *John Henry* (Caldecott Honor Book and *Boston Globe–Horn Book Award*), *Sam and the Tigers,* and most recently, *When the Beginning Began* and *What a Truly Cool World.* He is a professor of Judaic studies and adjunct professor of English and history at the University of Massachusetts, Amherst. He and his wife live in western Massachusetts.

Chris Lynch is the author of several novels, including *Shadow Boxer, Gypsy Davey,* and *Slot Machine,* as well as the "He-Man Women Haters Club" series. His most recent books are *Extreme Elvin,* and the forthcoming *Whitechurch.*

Harry Mazer's numerous books for young readers are read both in this country and abroad. *Snow Bound* received Second German TV network's "Preis der Lesseratten" and is on *Booklist*'s List of Contemporary Classics. *The New York Times Book Review* called *The Last Mission* one of the best books of the year and the American Library Association included it in its "Best of the Best" Books, 1970–1983. *When the Phone Rang* received Western Australia's Young Readers Award. His most recent books are *The Dog in the Freezer, The Wild Kid,* and a collection of gun stories, *Twelve Shots,* that he edited.

Norma Fox Mazer is the author of two short-story collections and twenty-four novels, for which she has received numerous awards, including the Edgar, two Lewis Carroll Shelf Awards, the Christopher Award, a National Book Award nomination, and a Newbery Honor. She has coedited a collection of women's poetry and contributed short stories to many anthologies. She's proud to be included in this one. Her most recent book is *When She Was Good,* and her novel *Mrs. Fish, Ape, and Me the Dump Queen* was recently re-released as *Crazy Fish.*

Walter Dean Myers's first fifty books have earned him four Coretta Scott King Awards, two Newbery Honors, and the Margaret Edwards Award. He is currently working on the next fifty books under the supervision of his wife and her six-toed cat.

Katherine Paterson is the author of more than twenty-five books, including twelve novels for young people. Two of these novels are National Book Award winners: *The Master Puppeteer* (1977) and *The Great Gilly Hopkins* (1979). She also received the Newbery Medal in 1978 for *Bridge to Terabithia* and again in 1981 for *Jacob Have I Loved*. Her latest novel is *Jip, His Story,* the winner of the 1997 Scott O'Dell Award for Historical Fiction. Her books have been published in twenty-two languages, and she is the 1998 recipient of the international Hans Christian Andersen Medal.

Susan Beth Pfeffer is the award-winning author of more than sixty books for children and young adults. Among her many titles are *About David, The Year Without Michael, Family of Strangers,* and *Twice Taken*. Ms. Pfeffer lives in Wallkill, New York.

Rachel Vail writes novels for adolescents. She is the author of *Wonder, Do Over* (in which Jody and Mackey first appear, as eighth-graders), *Ever After,* and *Daring to Be Abigail,* as well as the sequence of novels called "The Friendship Ring." She lives in New York City with her husband and son, and is active in both the Authors Guild and nursery school. She lovingly dedicates this story to her Aunt Tillie.

Jacqueline Woodson is the author of a number of books for children, young adults, and adults, including *I Hadn't Meant to Tell You This, Lena, If You Come Softly,* and *From the Notebooks of Melanin Sun*. She is the recipient of two Coretta Scott King Honors and two Jane Addams Peace Award honors.

Paul Zindel is the author of many novels for young readers, such as *The Pigman, The Undertaker's Gone Bananas,* and *My Darling, My Hamburger.* His recent adventures into the Zone Unknown include such horror/thrillers as *Loch, The Doom Stone,* and *Raptor.* He won the Pulitzer Prize for his play *The Effects of Gamma Rays on Man-in-the-Moon Marigolds* and has written the screenplays for *Up the Sandbox, Mame,* and *Runaway Train.*